THE GENTLEMEN'S CLUB

A Story for All Women

by

Becky Due

TELEMACHUS PRESS

Cover Designed by Craig Van Wechel of VW Design

Author Photo by Dennis Jones Photography

Published by Telemachus Press, LLC
http://www.telemachuspress.com

Visit the author website:
http://www.BeckyDue.com

Library of Congress Control Number: 2012948303

ISBN: 978-1-938701-46-7 (eBook)
ISBN: 978-1-938701-47-4 (Paperback)

Version 2012.09.24

Printed in the United States of America

10 9 8 7 6 5 4 3 2 1

THE GENTLEMEN'S CLUB

Chapter 1

I FELT ON edge. I had a feeling things were about to change. I had been sleeping in the same parking lot too often, but it was my favorite. It belonged to a business with employees, twenty-four hours a day, seven days a week. Small hills surrounded my car, blocking me from the road. I felt safe being only slightly off the main highway. The same traffic that carried my danger also carried my security.

I changed into my sweats, the clothes I slept in. I watched a man walking toward my car from my side mirror. I quickly tried to rearrange my car so it wasn't obvious that I was living there. I grabbed my pen and paper and tried to look busy as if doing an assignment for college under the parking lot lights. I began thinking about what I would say to him.

Maybe he was coming to help.

He tapped on my driver's side window. I acted surprised and rolled it down a crack. I could tell by the disgust on his face that he was not there to help me.

"What are you doing here?" he asked.

"I…"

"You can't sleep here!"

"Oh, I'm not. I'm waiting for my workout partner. He's late. We workout at that gym," I said, pointing.

He knew I was lying and walked away.

I rolled up the window and tears rolled down my face. I was embarrassed. I was angry at him. Couldn't he see I was homeless? I just needed a safe place to sleep. I hardly drink. I don't do drugs. I'm not a dirty street person. I shower every day.

But to him, I was trash.

I couldn't stop crying. I drove my car to the public library to take my mind off my lonely homelessness. I couldn't go in. My tears wouldn't stop. I tried to laugh it off. It had worked in the past, but not this time. I was tired. I had beaten myself down. I was no longer a hard scab. I was an open wound and I was in pain. The cold hurt. The night hurt.

And every thought hurt.

After sitting in torment for two hours, I went to the dry cleaning store I managed and let myself inside. I grabbed the phone book and searched for a hotline for help. My eyes still blurry with tears, I dialed the number. The woman who answered connected me to a shelter. Within a half an hour, I was driving to that shelter for help.

Judith, a heavyset woman, led me to the dining room. We sat down together at the table. I was still crying.

"We have room. We'd like you to stay," Judith said.

"I really just want to talk to someone."

"OK. Can I get you something?"

"No," I said. "I was doing fine until tonight. A man kicked me out of a parking lot. All I wanted was a safe place to park my car so I could get some sleep. I wasn't breaking any laws, was I?" I asked, wanting to be reassured that I wasn't.

"Why are you living in your car, Angie? Do you have family?"

"Because I can't afford a place to live. And, yes, I have family but I can't be around them." I grabbed a Kleenex from the box in front of me, then added, "Not like this. I don't want to be around anyone right now."

"We can help you find a job."

"I have a job, two jobs," I snapped.

"Are you angry at me?"

I took a deep breath and sighed, remembering that this woman wanted to help me. "No… I'm just tired." My tears welled up again, and I put my head down on the table.

"Honey, why don't you stay with us tonight."

That thought frightened me. Who would I have to share a room with? Who would I have to talk to? Would I have to fill out paper work, let the government know I was homeless? Would I have to get up in the morning and do chores? Would I be safe? "I just want a safe place to park."

"OK. What about those twenty-four hour grocery stores. You could park at Cub Foods one night and Rainbow the next. There are enough people around that nobody should bother you. The parking lots are well lit, and I'm sure nobody would chase you out."

"That's a good idea," I said and raised my head. I had already spent many nights at those parking lots. It wasn't easy sleeping there. Besides the bright lights, I woke to many car doors slamming. It didn't matter where I parked in those lots; somebody always ended up right next to me. I often heard them talking about me, reminding me what I had become.

"Angie, if you have two jobs, why are you living in your car?"

"Well, I was living with a guy. We were both miserable, so I moved out. I have credit card debt. I owe more money each month than I make. I never found a place to live. I thought I'd live like this for a month or so just to get back on my feet, but it's five months later and I'm still here."

I felt the heat in my face and added, "I'm crying more… It's getting harder."

Judith spent three hours counseling me on money, relationships, and how to take better care of myself. The three areas I had been failing. She reassured me that no matter how far in debt I was, nobody had the right to keep me from a roof over my head.

Before I left the shelter around 2:00 a.m., Judith loaded me up with canned food, crackers, peanut butter, shampoo, tampons, and toothpaste. She helped me carry the two bags out to my car. Judith gave me a hug and told me to be safe. That was the first human touch I'd had in a long time. I missed being touched.

Chapter 2

I HAD MY favorite clothes hanging on the hook in the back seat area. My shoes, worn less often, were in a box in my hatch back. On the floor in the back seat, I had a duffel bag, which held my gym clothes, makeup, blow dryer, deodorant, and personal items. In the front seat on the floor next to me were my cases of music tapes, and on top of them were all my notebooks for writing and an extra pair of shoes. Behind the passenger seat hanging from the headrest was a plastic bag for garbage. Beneath it on the floor was my bag of dirty clothes.

My weekdays consisted of morning workouts at the gym and the use of the shower facility, followed by my eight-hour day at the dry cleaners where I worked. A nap usually followed because my nights were anywhere from four to five hours of restless sleep. Day sleep seemed a little safer.

I chose to park in parking lots of parks, apartment complexes, restaurants, or in nice neighborhoods. The daylight and the activity of people made it hard to sleep. On some days my nap involved nothing more than watching people and trying to relax. I would set my alarm clock for an hour or two and recline my seat. If I wasn't sleepy, I wrote, read, talked into my tape recorder, or listened to music and watched the world around me. I was never afraid during the day, just embarrassed.

I was an outsider. I tried to picture myself inside the restaurant with friends having lunch. I couldn't. I had no friends. I tried to picture myself at the park with my kids. I couldn't. I did not want to have children. I tried to pretend I was in front of my house and that I just came from the grocery store getting ready to prepare my husband's favorite meal. But I couldn't imagine that either. I wanted to get married, but I wasn't sure why. I wanted to love somebody and have somebody love me. I wanted to learn how to trust a man. I wanted to learn how to trust myself. I wanted that companionship with someone special.

When I did get to sleep during the day, my sleep was restless. When my alarm woke me, I was a little moody. I wanted more sleep. I would hit the four-minute snooze or reset the alarm for another thirty minutes. I think a lot of my moodiness was because I knew people could see me so vulnerable. I didn't want them to see me that way.

After my nap, I had a choice of several different activities. I usually went to the library or a restaurant for a diet Coke, where I would watch people and do some writing.

My weeknights were nothing more than finding a safe place to sleep. I had a few places, which were my favorites, but I had to move around a lot to avoid being chased away. I slept in the back seat of my 1990 Honda Civic DX 2-door hatchback.

Once I found a place where I felt safe, I locked my car doors and hung my clothes in the windows to block as much of the back seat from the outside as possible. I then rearranged everything in the back seat to make room for me. I pulled my sleeping bag from the hatch back and used my cloth bag of dirty clothes for a pillow. I reached under my seat for my knife and hammer and tossed them in the back seat on top of my sleeping bag.

After using a cleanser to wash my face, I brushed my teeth with a diluted diet Coke. I took my time to get ready for bed. I looked around a lot. I became familiar with my surroundings.

While getting ready for bed, I thought over what could happen to me while I was there and how I would react to each situation. At first, I slept with my car keys in hand. I feared that someone could break my window, jump in, and drive away before I knew what was happening. What if he didn't break my window? What if he just tapped on it to scare me and held a knife telling me to open the door? My first thought would be to jump in front with keys in hand and drive away. What if sleeping with my keys made them hard to find and I lost too much time looking for them? I placed them on the floor next to me.

I always parked so nobody could block me in. If they pulled in front of me, I could back out. If they stopped behind me, I could drive forward. I usually imagined one man in my car, one person I had to deal with. And as silly as it was to think this way, I felt that I could talk to him and he would not hurt me. Not talking about God, trying to help him see the light and him crying to me about his problems. Not by telling him I will do anything he asks or by waiting for a moment to escape. In these fantasies, I never thought of leaving my home or letting someone take it. Or by leaving the situation or letting him have me. My thoughts were of a writer wanting adventure in any form that I could get it. Being down on my luck just like whoever it is that decides to try to take something from me.

What if I did open the door to him whether he had a knife or not and before he has a chance to say anything I ask, "So what are we going to do? Go rob a convenience store?" And if my talking didn't work, I'd probably still be in the back seat after being knocked around for a while, my hammer in view on the floor. He drives my car, and I wait for him to slow down enough with nothing to run into in case I can't get to the steering wheel in time. I reach for my hammer and wait. At the perfect moment, I strike him as hard as I can in the head, sending blood against my window. And I keep hitting until his movement stops. I don't hit to hurt him or to stop him from doing this; I hit him to kill him. Not to hit the surface of his head, but to go through it. If forced to sit in the front next to him, I would look afraid and lean my back against the door. I'd cry and he would feel confident it was from fear. But the tears would be from the anger that had built up inside me for years, because of the way I've seen women treated, because of the way I was treated. This man dared to enter my world. This man would become my victim. Unable to get my hammer or knife, again I would wait. I'd wait for that moment to kick my feet through his head and through the driver's door window. Then I'd grab my knife and stab his neck over and over again until he's almost beheaded, turning my blue interior red. I'd do this for one reason and one reason only, because he violated me. Maybe he didn't rape me or steal from me, but he looked at me as lesser or weaker than him. Why? Because I'm a woman? Because he thinks, he can? Well, he can't! He may have done the same thing to me if I had given him the chance.

By the time I was ready for bed, I had to go to the bathroom. I grabbed the same cup I spit in, after brushing my teeth. I pulled my pants and underwear down while I moved to the edge of my seat. I held the cup under my legs next to the seat, and peed into it. When finished I looked around to see if I felt safe opening my door. I unlocked it, opened it, poured my urine onto the pavement and watched it steam as I close and locked my door. If I was already in my sweats, I was ready for bed. If not I changed into them, so I wouldn't have to in the morning before my workout.

After performing my nightly ritual and checking the door locks one more time, I would retreat to my sleeping bag in the back seat. I would get as comfortable as the cramped space would allow. Like every night I would reach for my tape recorder and talk. It was company before I slept, and I felt the last words at night were worth recording for reference to my life. If I didn't survive the night and my tape recorder was found, maybe my family would understand more about me and my life and how I was truly happy, though struggling.

Chapter 3

ONE SATURDAY MORNING after an hour on the Stairmaster, I headed to the women's locker room to get ready for my day. There were not a lot of women around on this weekend morning. It seemed I had the place to myself. I tried to use the gym at less busy hours, not only for the use of the equipment, but also for the use of the locker room. I have been modest with my body most my life. I always used the same shower stall: the one farthest back against the wall and out of sight of the women's locker area.

I was in the shower letting the warm water fully cover my hair and body. The steam relaxed me even more. I wanted to take my time, but I also wanted to finish before the locker room filled. I looked down to the soap dispenser as I pulled the lever forward. It was empty.

I peeked out of my shower door to see if anyone was around. The coast was clear, so naked and dripping I stepped out and opened the door of the other shower stall. I grabbed a few squirts of the pink liquid soap and rushed back to my shower where the warm water was still running. I noticed the mess of water I'd made on the floor tile, only happy I'd gotten away with it without anyone seeing me.

Once my shower was over and the water was off, I was confident I had the place to myself. The only sound was an occasional slamming of weights and the music playing in the gym area. I stood next to my shower stall, in the pool of water on the floor and dried off. Something told me to look up and as I did, I saw the sauna door was open a crack. I pulled my towel to cover myself as I gasped for air. A man had been standing behind that door watching me. I felt violated and scared. I didn't understand why a man would do this to me. I wondered if it had become acceptable behavior in our society, or was it because he felt he could get away with it.

After investigating, I discovered the window on the coed sauna door on the women's side was a clear view into our locker room. I looked into the men's window and could only see a white wall. I was disgusted. The manager was not available on the weekend, so I had to wait until Monday to talk to him. I didn't. Instead, I decided to find a different gym.

Chapter 4

ON FRIDAY NIGHTS, I usually would go to a restaurant lounge where I sipped a diet Coke or a beer. I watched all the people, everyone in pairs or a group. I'd sit alone in a booth with my notebook and pen. I sometimes wrote about the people around me, what I imagined their lives to be like. I usually wrote about me; why I was alone, why I was homeless, and why I wanted to keep it that way for a while. If I wasn't careful, my desire to write dissolved while getting high from my beer. Then I wanted to either go out dancing or sleep. But because I was afraid to drive, I stayed until the buzz wore off. Those were the times true loneliness set in.

I was often led to strike up conversations with strangers. I would stop to pay for my gas at the convenience store before going to a bar and then stay and talk to the guy working the midnight shift. He was younger than I was and his level of conversation showed it. But I was lonely, and he was willing to talk.

There was a guy who came in to pay for his gas and said he was driving around with a stray cat under his hood. I went out to look and I couldn't see it. To assure me it was there, he crawled under the car to scare it away then started yelling, "There it goes did you see it?" I didn't see a thing.

Once a young man came in and asked me if I wanted to go dancing at the Mega Mall with him and his friend. I looked out and saw another guy in the truck. I told him I would follow them. I love to dance, but I was having a nice time hanging out in the gas station. I decided not to go.

The guy at the gas station thought I was as strange as every other customer who came in, and I probably was. I would leave him around eleven and head on to my destination to write.

On weekends, I'd go for drives and stop when I found a place I liked. Then I'd write or get out and go for a walk. On those drives, I talked into my tape recorder about my life, my struggles, or anything I felt was important at the time.

I only left town to do my laundry, which was my only responsibility on the weekends. I could do it anywhere I found a Laundromat. I went to places all over the Midwest and northern areas. These were good times in places I'd never been. I loved the differences in the people.

If I didn't do my laundry out of town, I would do it at the local twenty-four hour Laundromat. It was a good place to go at night because almost everything in the area was open twenty-four hours. It was just off a highway and usually used by truckers. There was a McDonalds, a convenience store and gas station, and a few other places to eat. Any business that was open all the time was a good place for me to be at night.

I slept well in the hotel parking lots. Plus, by ten o'clock, hotel halls gave me a place to eat. I would walk the floors looking for room service trays or pizza boxes. The usual was half a sandwich, pizza, bread, or soggy fries. I was careful. I looked the food over before I ate it, and I kept walking. After my late dinner, I'd head to my car to go to sleep.

Chapter 5

I OFTEN WENT out on Saturday nights to an underground bar in downtown Minneapolis. I didn't drink when I was there. I felt it would be too dangerous: a woman alone, possibly a little buzzed. I knew I would not be as alert if I had a drink. I didn't talk to anyone. I was there to dance and watch the people. There were gays and lesbians so far out of the closet they were out of the house. I saw drugs and half-naked people every time I went there.

I tried to get there early so I could get my spot, which was a small platform with a pole going from the floor to the ceiling. I made sure to get it every night I went. I danced for three to four hours until I had to go to the bathroom, which meant losing my position on the dance floor. If that were the case, I walked around and watched people.

There was strange art all over, sculptures and paintings. It was dark and dingy, with the main light coming from the huge fish tank by the front door. There were balconies where people could stand out of the way and watch the dancing from different levels. I went to the same bar every time to get a glass of water. There were loose nails under the bar with a glass cover. If you pressed your hand under it, against the nails, you could see its form through the glass. It entertained me while I waited.

On several nights when I was there, men would stand around me as I danced on the platform. They often tried to hand me money as if I were a stripper. A few times, I had men come up to me and want to shake my hand before leaving. They would tell me how much they enjoyed watching me dance and how my being there made their night.

One time a man and woman came over to meet me and shake my hand, but it was different. It was the night of the fight. I had been dancing alone and two drunk guys started jumping up on my platform trying to dance with me. They were average looking, in their mid-twenties. I was not in the mood for company, nor did I want to share my platform with them. I asked them to find a different place to dance. They were feeling sure of themselves. The alcohol made them invincible.

Instead of finding another woman to harass, they kept after me. They slam danced into me, almost knocking me off the platform. Hanging onto the pole was the only thing keeping me up. I was getting pissed. Every time they came to my platform, I'd push them off. It led to more aggressiveness on their part, but I didn't care, I was standing my ground.

The blonde-haired guy, who was most aggressive, came up again and threw a punch. I moved back just in time to catch it in the shoulder instead of the face. It still hurt. My reaction was to hit back, but he had already turned his back, about to hop off, so I punched him in the back. His hand reached for the pain.

He took off but his friend stayed. I yelled to him over the music, "I'm here to dance and I'm not bothering anyone. Will you tell your friend to quit bothering me."

"I'll try," he yelled back and walked off.

Every bouncer in the club was huge and muscular, so when one came over by me to pick up glasses and empty bottles I asked him to keep an eye out for me. I was unsure of what the two guys might do. "There are two guys who are really bugging me," I yelled above the booming base.

Before I could finish, he said, "Well, if you didn't dance so sexy maybe you wouldn't have that problem."

"It's not like that. The guy hit me!"

"Some guy hit you?"

"Yes."

"Where is he? Point him out."

I looked around but couldn't see them. "I don't know where they are. Just keep an eye out, OK?"

"I will. And I'll tell the other guys, too."

"OK, thanks." I did not see them again until later, but they didn't bother me.

That is when the couple came over and said I had made their night. I shook their hands and thought if I had been watching it, I would have been amused too, seeing a woman stand her ground with a couple of drunk assholes.

When it was getting late and I was tired, I'd prepare myself before I walked out of the club. I left before the bar closed to avoid the crowds of drunk people. On the walk to the parking ramp, my senses were sharp, but it was my intuition that guided me. A couple times I turned around and walked back in to the club. Not because I heard or saw something, but because I felt the need to. Then I'd wait for a couple to leave and follow them to the ramp and to my car.

I would quickly check the back seat while unlocking my door, jump in, and lock the door behind me. Home at last, I'd think to myself. I would start my car and drive away yawning.

It was a twenty-minute drive to the suburb of my choice. Tired of music, I'd keep the radio off. The buzzing in my ears promoted thoughts about my life. Sometimes I reached for my recorder to talk to myself. I liked myself, though I was often confused. I thought I was funny, interesting, and a blast to be with.

After finding a place to park and getting ready for bed, I continued to talk into my tape recorder until I fell asleep.

"Oh, what a life I lead… I'm sure I burned at least three calories tonight dancing, maybe even four. Oh I'm so tired…uh…ahmmm (Yawn)." I grabbed my alarm clock and pressed the light button. "Let's see what time it is. Oh, my goodness, it's 123 1:23. It would be even cooler if it was 1234, but then I wouldn't be here yet and I'm happy being here. Oh…uh…ahmmm (yawn) I should get to sleep." I rolled over onto my side and put the recorder on the seat next to my face. "What am I going to do? I can't live like this forever." The thought of that man watching me in the locker room infuriated me. I could feel the knot of anger in my chest and I pushed it down, burying it. "Maybe I should just go be a stripper. My body isn't that bad. I love to dance. I love music. The guys seem to like me.

Maybe I'd be good at it. I mean if guys want to see me naked and they're going to find a way to look anyway, maybe I should at least be paid for it… yeah, I should. I don't want to be a stripper though… let's see… what… do I want… to be? Let's see… I want to be a writer… I want to be a writer…"

Chapter 6

THEN BLAKE CAME into my life. At first, he was kind and fun to be with. He had roommates, so after the movie or going out for dinner, we usually went to a hotel to spend time together alone. We would watch television, go swimming, and make love.

He knew how I was living, so he paid for everything. And before he left, he would give me money. It started with my car needing new brakes, so he gave me money to take care of them and it went from there. I don't remember how I got so dependent on him and the situation, but I do remember the last time:

I was driving to the hotel, thinking about how my life led me to this point. I thought about the last time Blake and I spoke.

"Angie, let me get you a beeper."

I was shocked, "A beeper? Why?"

"I can't get a hold of you unless you're at the dry cleaners, and you're only there 'til four," he said. "What if around six I decide I want to take you to a movie?"

"I guess you'll have to get in the habit of asking me in advance." I was trying to be cute, but I could not deny the burning lump in my throat. We didn't go to movies anymore; we went to hotels. I was hurt. I was not going to be on call for a man, just like a prostitute.

Before I fell into overwhelming sadness, I escaped from myself, completely becoming somebody else, something else.

I pulled up to the hotel where we were to meet. I didn't see his car, so I drove around the parking lot to reassure myself he was not there yet. I was late as always. I looked around for a place to park. I noticed a spot in the shade, under a tree, so I pulled in. It was hot, about a hundred degrees outside. I turned my key enough so I could listen to the radio. It was already on the jazz station I wanted to listen to, so I leaned my seat back to enjoy the music more comfortably. I glanced at my clock to check the time; he was late, too. The real me who was hiding behind the protective shield was hoping that I had missed him. Suddenly, my favorite song was playing on the radio; the one that made me happy about life.

I was trying to figure out a way to escape. The person I had become kept pushing me back into hiding so she could go through with it, so she could get needed money in her pocket. At twelve minutes after three, he pulled up in his fancy car. He handed me a hundred and seventy dollars cash and told me to go in and get the seventy-dollar room. The hundred was for me. I was happy to have it in my hand. I walked into the hotel to pay for the room.

I filled out the card and the clerk asked, "Cash or credit card?"

"Cash," I said.

She had to see my driver's license, and of course, I didn't bring it in. I left the money on the counter and headed out to my car.

"Did you get it?" he asked.

"No. I need my ID. You'd think I'd know this by now," I said. "Oh, and I never did get the condoms. Do you want to get them while I get the room?"

"Yeah, OK. I'll meet you back here."

"OK."

I ran back in and gave her my identification. She checked it and handed it back to me along with my change and key. I walked back to my car.

He walked up to me. "I got them. Did you get the room all right?" he asked.

"Yeah. Let's park around back," I said.

We walked upstairs, and some people were coming down. I wondered what they were thinking. It was clear Blake and I were not a match. I'm attractive, but it was obvious when you looked at me I was not loaded with money. On the other hand, when you looked at him, it was obvious he was.

Once we walked into our room and shut the door, the tension dissolved. We were alone. I threw down my bag and jumped onto the bed. I started jumping as I watched him turn on the television. He was tall with the body of a swimmer. He turned toward me and said the same thing he always said, "Aren't hotels great?"

I smiled and stopped jumping. "Talk shows," I said, as he flipped through the channels.

He found one that looked good and turned to me to check for my approval. He walked over to me, handed me a beer, and gave me a kiss. At that point, I always felt like a child, knowing he had complete control over me.

I didn't like talk shows much, but when I was with him, it seemed appropriate. We lay on the bed and laughed in disbelief at the topics, guests, and the things being said, both knowing we could be there ourselves.

By now, I had a little buzz from my beer, and he wanted me. He rolled toward me and kissed me. At that moment, I could not stand him. He was telling me how beautiful I was, how perfect my body was, and how badly he wanted me. His breath, matching his words, disgusted me. He was kissing me and touching me, but it wasn't me. I was inside crying while the protective me was trying to ignore the reality of what was taking place. She was fantasizing. She was pretending it was not happening, yet fantasizing that it was. She was trying to enjoy the moment.

"Put it on," he said.

I reached over to the nightstand, grabbed the gold condom package, tore it open and tossed it to the floor. He smiled at me; what else could I do but smile back. He rolled us over; lying on top of me, he tried to excite me. The television was more exciting to me.

When it was over and he was gone, I was alone to face my guilt and question my morals. I looked around the room at my wet swimming suit, the empty beer cans, condom wrappers, and the dishes on trays from the room service we had ordered. I felt so alone. I sat on the unmade bed and tried to put a smile on my face. I tried to regain my strength by telling myself it wasn't that bad. I just spent the night with an attractive man and got a hundred dollars in the process. With this thought, the tears started coming. With my elbows on my knees, I raised my hands to catch my falling head. I knew living this lie was destroying me.

After a good cry, it was time to go. I collected my things and headed for the door. I stood with my hand on the doorknob. I turned back and looked the room over. Emotionless, I opened the door and walked down the hallway. I heard the door close and latch behind me, a symbol of that chapter of my life. I welcomed a chill throughout my body. I closed my eyes; I knew that was the last time.

Chapter 7

MY PART-TIME JOB was to help pay my bills and to kill time. I cleaned city hall, for a company contracted to clean office buildings, from six to eleven p.m. Monday, Wednesday, and Friday. I loved working there. With hip-hop on my Walkman, I kept moving. In time, to keep from getting too hot, I would remove my sweatshirt revealing the T-shirt I'd worn beneath it. I saw cleaning not as a dreaded job, but a great aerobic workout.

The woman who had trained me told me stories about a man named Bob, who would harass her. She believed he was the city attorney or city manager, she wasn't sure. She claimed he was harmless but worked late and always wanted to talk to her, telling her she was pretty and keeping her from her work.

I wasn't as nice. Besides making my job more fun, my Walkman kept the man from talking to me. I was always careful when I was on his side of the building. I didn't dance around; I just did my job. On the other side, I cut loose. I made it fun.

I remember being in the women's bathroom with Aaliyah playing on my Walkman. I finished cleaning the toilets, emptying the garbage canisters in the stalls, the worst part of my job, and wiping down the stalls. While cleaning the sink area, I danced around lip synching, looking at myself in the mirror. I tried to look sexy. I tucked the bottom of my shirt through the neck to expose my stomach and some of my upper chest, where cleavage would be if I had larger breasts. I pulled my long brown hair up on my head the way I've seen women do on music videos and TV and wondered if I had what it takes to be a star. My body was average but with more muscle tone than most. I pulled my sleeves up on my shoulders while cleaning the floor to admire my biceps and triceps pushing and pulling the wet mop. Before leaving the bathroom I'd adjust my shirt and give myself one last look. It was nice to be alone to look at myself. I never felt comfortable looking at myself in the women's locker room at the gym for fear women would walk in and catch me.

That night I was finished cleaning and struggling to get the mop bucket past the heavy bathroom door. Bob was standing there leaning against the wall. Watching me but not offering me help. It scared me. He began talking to me, but I didn't remove my head set, so I couldn't hear him. I just pointed to my ears and proceeded to push the bucket down the hall to the front of the building. I was embarrassed. I feared he might have been watching me looking at myself in the bathroom mirror, trying to be sexy. God, please don't let him have been watching me.

Two weeks after working there, I went to the office of the company who hired me to pick up my first check. The large bearded man in charge of the cleaning service told me he had to talk to me, so I followed him into his office and he shut the door.

"I've had a strange complaint about you. You're doing great cleaning. What you have been wearing is the problem," he said.

"I thought it was OK if I wore sweats."

"I got a phone call. I was told you're wearing halter tops."

"What! I don't even own a halter top. I wear sweats and a T-shirt," I exclaimed.

"Well… he said he has important men there for night meetings, and he doesn't want them to pay more attention to the cleaning lady than to what the meeting is about," he said. "But if you say you're wearing T-shirts, well OK, then."

"Forget it! I quit." I walked out of his office with my check. I was furious. Bob had no right to open the women's bathroom door. The only reason I was in trouble was that I wouldn't give him attention. I remembered all the times he tried to talk to me. My short talks with Bob consisted of nothing more than, "I like your top." or, "What kind of music do you listen to?"

I wanted to give up.

Chapter 8

THE FIRST SNOW of the season was amazing. I woke with a smile when I realized a blanket of sparkles had covered my car. I felt lucky to be exposed, one with Mother Nature.

I loved the snowfall at night. It made my sleep easier. I began to believe that God was tucking me in at night with the heavy white blanket. I felt protected from the world.

Deeper into winter, depression was moving in. I believe the main cause was shortness of sleep. It was getting colder. The snow was still welcome, but the freezing air was not. The romance of the snow had shifted to finding understanding and acceptance.

I chose to believe God made it snow for me alone, for my protection. Maybe God saw a man in trouble looking to cause trouble for someone else. I could imagine him stirring inside himself sitting in his house angry at the world or women. God watches and knows what could happen so decides to throw me a blizzard. The snow comes down while I'm sleeping. I lay peaceful in my sleeping bag, tape recorder lying by my face, still running. The man leaves his house with his snow boots on but no coat. He needs to vent some anger; he needs to hurt someone. He wants his own pain to stop. He is walking fast, so God dumps the snow a little faster. By the time the man walks by, snow has completely covered my car. He didn't even know I was there and passes me by. God looks down and a smile of relief fills me and that man who walked long enough to blow off the steam. He punched a tree a few times and threw snowballs at a sign.

Or maybe the weather was too cold for that man to leave his house so he goes downstairs and lifts weights instead. I wake, believing in *that* reason for the snow and cold weather, and I thank God, no matter how hard it was on me.

It took that kind of faith to get through each freezing night. I was becoming numb in the cold and faith in myself was fading. I tried to find meaning in what this winter was bringing to me. Everything dead and frozen matched how I felt about myself. I wasn't crying as much. I had no feeling. I wasn't embarrassed anymore, and I did not feel sorry for myself. It was just the way it was. I was in hell and I had to deal with it.

Every winter night had the same routine. I drove around with my heat blaring until I found a place to park. I kept my car running until I was ready to go to sleep. I crawled in back with my sleeping bag and two blankets I had picked up. The desperation tried to take me over; it tried to cause tears. It would be another sleepless night. My backseat bed couldn't keep me warm enough. I wanted to call Blake. It didn't matter how I felt in that relationship. I wanted company, I wanted warmth, and I wanted a bed to sleep in.

I adjusted my back seat, tucked myself in and buried my head under the covers. I couldn't leave my skin exposed. I lay fantasizing about having a great apartment.

I wanted ceiling fans, Venetian blinds, and a fireplace. I would have all new comfortable furniture, a king-size bed with a big white down comforter. I wanted to be like the businesswomen who came into the dry cleaners. They had nice clothes, perfect hair and nails, and they always left the scent of expensive perfume. Some were married, some weren't, but they all had beautiful diamond rings. I wanted to be one of those women dropping my clothes off at the dry cleaners on my way to work. I wanted lots of friends. I would entertain at my apartment. I wanted a great boy friend. Someday, I would get a cat to lie by the fireplace.

Within three hours, I was still in my sleeping bag, but sitting in the front seat with the car running. The cold air from the vents felt warm to me. I sat under the parking lot lights half asleep and shivering. I scratched at the white layer of frost that had accumulated on my sleeping bag in that short amount of time.

The heat was thawing part of my windshield so I reclined my seat. I was too far from the heat so I sat back up. I tried to relax but not enough to sleep. I feared falling asleep with my car running. I imagined snow packed in my muffler causing the exhaust to back up into my car. I did not want to die like that. I didn't want anyone to question if it had been suicide.

Sometimes I drove around at two in the morning to warm the engine. I needed the heat to go back to sleep. After my first wake up, I always stayed in the front reclined seat to sleep. Several car warm-ups always followed, about every two hours.

After several nights of freezing, I snapped. I could see no other way out. I decided to replace the night job I just quit with being a stripper. The money I'd make would get me into an apartment, get me some nice clothes, and I would be warm and have friends. Instead of men finding me a nuisance in our society and chasing me out of parking lots, they would find me attractive and want me around.

Chapter 9

I HAD BEEN to several different clubs around the Minneapolis area and found only one where I felt I could dance. The building was long and narrow. When you first walked in it looked like a dinner club. Past the dividing wall was the bar where the dancing took place. There were three stages, a large one in the center and two smaller floors off to each side. There were stools around all three stages for men who wanted to tip.

The dancing was not completely nude. The g-string stayed on and the music wasn't bad. One thing I didn't like was not having a choice of music. I wanted to choose. I was fussy when it came to the type of music I wanted to dance to, but I felt I could pull it off.

I had my interview and auditioned on the same day. The interview was nothing more than the boss telling me what he expected of me. He was tall and stocky, wearing a black turtle neck and sport coat. He informed me that many women wanted to dance there and if I wasn't on time or called in sick, he would have to let me go. He took me in back and introduced me to the other dancers who were working that afternoon. He told them if I didn't have something to wear, they should help me out. The dancers were nice but totally checking me out. I started changing into my own outfit, a slinky black dress, black pumps, and a black bra and g-string set. The boss came back in and said, "You look great. Are you ready?"

"Yeah, I guess so." I was nervous. I followed him out to the middle stage. He hopped off and sat with two other guys, the owner and a bouncer. There were about five other guys at various tables spread out in the club. They appeared to be on their lunch breaks from painting, construction, sales, and court.

The music started and so did I. I ignored everyone and let the song take me. I didn't dance much different than I would have at my favorite club, but every feeling inside me was different. What I was doing scared me.

When the song was over, I was hired. He brought me back and introduced me to the dancers again, this time as a new dancer. They welcomed me this time much more warmly. Some of them had watched me dance and said I was good. While I was changing back into my street clothes the boss came in, handed me a key to my locker, and said I was to start the next night.

An older dancer with long brown hair said, "Wow! If you're starting at night you must be good."

Another said, "She is." She was a young blonde who told all the men she was putting herself through college. She was really a single mother just trying to support her son. She said the college story made the guys feel less guilty, and so they tipped better.

They started talking to me about what to expect. The older woman told me how she got in trouble for putting ice on her nipples while on stage. She said you can't play with yourself or touch yourself while dancing. They explained how the men could not touch us either. We had to take the money from them; they couldn't put it in our g-string. The bouncers kicked men out for touching the dancers. The women tried to make me think that the dancers were protected.

They usually started the girls in the afternoon because the night crowd was harder. They started me on a Tuesday night. The place was busier than I thought. The music I danced to was good, but I was nervous. I didn't move around on the stage the way I should have. I was in front of two guys who seemed to like me, so I pretended I was dancing to them alone and it became easier for me. They looked like the type of guys who work construction, play softball on weekends and do a lot of drinking. I took their tips, and they kept repeating the same thing over and over again, "You got it… you got it, baby."

On one of my breaks, I was sitting at the bar, and a man who wanted to be my agent approached me. He was scruffy with long bushy dark hair.

He bought me a drink and gave me his card. He said I had a lot of talent and could go far. I played along. He told me he represented one of the dancers, and he got a man to buy her a new car. I played dumb. "Really! Wow, that's great!" I had to go back on stage so I excused myself and told him I'd call.

I spent my last break in the back. The highest paid dancer, from tips, a black-haired, breasty woman also thought I had a lot of talent. It seemed she also wanted to be my agent. She wanted to give me some lessons on moving around the stage and suggested I lose twenty pounds. She believed I would be the best one out there if I followed her advice. She was the woman who got a new car. I thanked her and left. I walked out to my home in the parking lot and never went back to dance again.

What I realized that night is that I had stopped caring about women and started caring more about men. I had been living in somebody else's fantasy of what a woman should be. It was time I figured out what I should be, not according to women and especially not according to men. I had hit bottom, but I knew I was on my way up. I was unsure how I would do it.

Chapter 10

I STARTED BY looking through the paper for an affordable apartment to rent or someone looking for a roommate. I called a man who was renting out his basement. He had two rooms rented and had one left. I would have to share the bathroom and kitchen with two men. It would be $150.00 a month, plus phone. I arranged to meet him right away.

He showed me the room. The floor was only half covered with the typical multi colored basement carpet. The rest was cold, damp cement. The two outer brick walls were pink. The other two walls were thin white drywall. There was a three-inch gap from ceiling to floor by the entrance to the room. The bathroom was dirty. Spider webs covered the walls and ceiling. The kitchen matched the rest of the musty basement.

"I'll take it," I said reaching in my pocket for the first month's rent.

I could tell he was surprised. He went upstairs to get the month-to-month lease and my keys. While alone I began to feel an ache in my chest. I wanted to cry from my accomplishment. I could not believe I had a place to live—a place to hang my clothes, a place to stretch out and sleep behind a locked door, a place where nobody could kick me out.

With keys in hand and the signed lease, I excitedly drove to my appointment to meet with a financial advisor. In my mind I imagined how I would decorate, where I would put my bed, once I got one. I knew I would buy a stereo, and I would put it under the window. I was excited to get a phone, and my own telephone number. I would get another job, a better job, now that I would have a way for people to contact me.

His name was Francis. He greeted me with a handshake, and we went into his office. We made a list of my monthly bills: rent, car payment, phone, and credit card debt. Then we figured out my income. While he ran my credit check, he gave me a budget worksheet to fill out. When I was finished, I handed it to him. He briefly glanced at it and said, "This is unrealistic."

I was ashamed and began to cry. "I need to file bankruptcy, don't I?"

"Oh, no. No. No. No." He said shaking his head. "This is going to be so easy on you. You just didn't give yourself enough freedom money. You need some fun money, eating out money, spending money," he said cheerfully.

I smiled, not completely believing him.

He began asking me questions regarding how I feel about money, what I like to do with my free time. He wanted to know how I liked to spend money.

Sadly, I didn't know. To me his questions were unanswerable. Before I was homeless, I used money—well, credit cards—to run away. I liked to get in my car and drive. I would stay in a hotel, order room service, go swimming and walk around the new city. I tried to forget my life.

Everything was different now. I didn't know what I'd want to buy. I knew I didn't want to run anymore. I began to open up and told him about being homeless.

He said he was very proud of me not only for getting a place to live, but also for getting help with my bills. His last question was "I bet when you get a bill in the mail and you know you can't afford to pay it, you go to the store and buy yourself something instead."

"How did you know?"

"It's common." He gave me a comforting smile. "What do you buy?"

"CDs," I answered.

"OK, then we need to give you a CD allowance."

"Let's see what we have here." He began writing on my budget sheet. "OK, you have three major credit cards: two Visa and one Master Card…all with a $500.00 credit limit. That's good. But they are maxed causing high interest and because they are over the $500.00 limit they are tacking on penalty fees. Now, you have three gas cards and four departments store cards… all pretty much maxed. Are you willing to cut up all your cards?" he kept his head down only raising his eyes causing his forehead to squint.

"Yes."

"OK, now, what we do, is send each of your creditors a letter stating that you've come to us for help. We ask them to lower the interest rate or stop charging it all together until the card is paid off. I'll tell you right now the Visa and Master Card will not work with us. The other companies most likely will. Therefore, we will be paying the major credit cards first, meaning they will be getting the larger payments from us. The others will get about five dollars a month. Once we pay off the high interest cards, then we will disburse more money to the others. Any questions?"

"Not yet."

"I know it doesn't sound like much, but trust me, it is."

He was right. I had hoped for a miracle.

"OK, now we need to figure out what you can pay us each month. Let's take a look at your budget plan together." He slid it my way so we could both see it, and he put a star next to rent, car payment, and phone. "We can't do anything about these. But these…" he smiled as he put a check mark by the credit card debts. "We can have some fun with these." He pulled the paper away from me again and said. "It looks like… $79.00 a month. How does that sound?"

There was the miracle. "You're kidding me? Wow! I can't believe that. Are you sure?"

"Yes, I'm sure."

"Can I pay more if I get a better job?"

"Absolutely. You can pay as much as you want but you *must* at least pay the $79.00. OK?"

"OK."

"We charge a one time fee of $25.00. We are nonprofit, but we charge you for stamps, envelopes, and the time to type up the letters and send them out. We also send you a statement every month to show you where your money is going. You pay us nothing now. We take a little of that $79.00 every month until we're paid. Any questions?"

"Yes. Will I still get bills in the mail?"

"Some you will, some you won't. It's up to you what you do with them. You can open them and take a look, or you can throw them away unopened. Most find it easier to just throw them away. But don't pay them."

"OK."

"OK, one more thing." He smiled. "Do you have your credit cards with you."

"Yes."

"Should we cut them up together?"

I reached for my bag and the tears welled up in my eyes. I was afraid to be responsible with my money. I was afraid to stop running from everything in my life. I was afraid of becoming normal and boring. I feared becoming the me I knew deep down I could be.

Chapter 11

I WELCOMED THE change I feared into my life as a friend to help me grow. It showed me a different type of strength of moving forward in positive ways, and it had a snowball effect, almost the exact opposite of the snowball effect of my life spiraling down in a negative path to nothing good.

They were small events that kept me looking for the next one to come along. I changed my address so I would receive my mail at my new home instead of the post office box, and the first envelope I opened was a letter from JC Penney. They congratulated me for getting the help with my bills and said they would no longer be charging me interest. The humiliation I had felt for being in this situation suddenly turned into pride. The company was respecting me now, not harassing me. I was proud of myself.

I had been sleeping on the floor in my sleeping bag for the past week. I decided it was time for a bed. The first garage sale I went to had a twin bed for ten dollars. I offered five and they took it. It took me two trips to haul the box spring and mattress to my place. I bought sheets, pillows and a comforter right away. I bought an extra mattress pad to protect me from some of the worn out springs. I set it up like a day bed. I loved my beautiful bed.

I had already cleaned my room, but it was time to clean the bathroom and kitchen. I also wanted to go to more garage sales to find some furniture. While cleaning the rest of the basement, I noticed a room by the bathroom that was full of junk. As I looked through it, I saw a few things I could use. There were some bricks and boards that I knew would make a cute shelf, and an old desk I wanted. I became excited and ran in to my room to call my landlord. He answered.

"Hi, this is Angie. I just moved in downstairs."

"Yes, Angie. How is everything?"

"Good. I've been cleaning and I noticed all that stuff in that room by the bathroom. Is it yours?" I asked excitedly.

"No. It's stuff other renters have left behind. I've been meaning to take it to the dump." He said. "Why?"

"Well, I was wondering if I could have a few things down there, like the desk and those bricks."

"Oh, sure, help yourself. But you better check with the other guys to see if they are storing anything in there."

"OK, I will. Thanks." I hung up and walked back by the kitchen to the other bedrooms. Tad was home and walked back to that room with me to look.

"No," he said. "The only thing that's mine are those weights. And I'm pretty sure nothin' back here belongs to John."

I couldn't help but take a look at him to see if he was a body builder. He must have been about 6'5", and he was husky. He was only a few years older than I was. Wearing a flannel shirt and jeans, he had that rugged out-doors look. His hair was blonde from the sun, not his parents or the beauty shop. I wasn't afraid of him. We became friends that day. He helped me carry the desk into my bedroom and even wiped off the spider webs for me.

Though we were both busy people, we knocked on each other's door often. He invited me to watch TV with him because I didn't have one. And sometimes I did. One night, I fell asleep in his room while watching a movie. I woke to him carrying me back to my own room and putting me on my bed. He turned around, turned the light off, locked my door handle and pulled the door shut as he left.

The gap in my wall also became handy. For me, I enjoyed sliding my hand in and turning my light on from the hall before I even unlocked my door. It was nice not to walk into a dark room and search for the light switch. For Tad, he liked to turn my light off when he got home from work, or he'd flick it off and on a few times like a strobe light. It was usually a sign that he wanted company.

I loved my place. My pet name for it was my pink prison cell. I wondered if it was the same pink painted in jail cells and holding tanks to relax the prisoners. My pink relaxed me. I was organized and clean. I had my bed, my stereo on my homemade shelf, and my desk. I picked up a desk chair at a garage sale and bought a bean bag chair on sale at Target.

I was on time. I paid my bills. I worked out at least four times a week. But most importantly, I was writing.

Chapter 12

THE POSITIVE SNOWBALL kept growing. I started taking an English class at the community college. That was huge for me because for so long I had feared I was too dumb to go school. I thought they would never let me in.

But I got in.

I went to the college the day before class started to be sure I could find my classroom, the bathrooms, and vending machines. "You don't belong," my body kept telling me. "You don't fit in." But my head kept saying, "I'll try. I'll just try."

After two weeks of 100 percent on all my papers, I decided to write my first piece for people to read.

I had gone back to the gym where the man looked at me from the sauna. I paid five dollars for the day pass and went straight into the locker room and to the sauna. It was the same. I went back to the front desk and asked to talk to the manager. He was in a back office and came up. I told him what I found. He said he would take care of it. One week later I went back; nothing had changed.

I wrote a letter to the women in the locker room and took it to my teacher to have her check for mistakes. I explained the whole situation. She corrected a few things and said she was proud of me for doing this.

The manager told me he would straighten it out but never did, so I decided to help him. I posted this letter all over the women's locker room.

ATTENTION LADIES: PLEASE READ!

I'M A WOMAN WHO WORKS OUT HERE. NOT LONG
AGO I WAS TAKING A SHOWER IN THE WOMEN'S
LOCKER ROOM. AS I WAS STANDING DRYING OFF,
SOMETHING TOLD ME TO LOOK UP. I RAISED MY
HEAD AND SAW THE SAUNA DOOR OPENED A
CRACK. THERE WAS A MAN WATCHING ME. I WAS
NAKED. THAT MAN TOOK SOMETHING AWAY FROM
ME THAT DAY. WHEN I NOTICED HE WAS THERE, HE
QUICKLY LEFT THE SAUNA AND WENT INTO THE
MEN'S LOCKER ROOM.

AFTER I FINISHED DRYING OFF AND PUTTING ON
MY CLOTHES, I WENT INTO THE SAUNA. I LOOKED
THROUGH THE WINDOW ON THE MEN'S SIDE, AND
ALL I COULD SEE WAS A WHITE WALL. ALREADY
KNOWING WHAT I WOULD FIND, I LOOKED
THROUGH THE WOMEN'S SIDE. SURE ENOUGH, I
COULD CLEARLY SEE RIGHT INTO THE WOMEN'S
LOCKER ROOM!

I TALKED TO THE MANAGER. HE PROMISED HE'D
TAKE CARE OF IT. A WEEK LATER AND NOTHING
HAS BEEN DONE. STILL, THE WINDOW IS BARE AND
SO ARE WE (IN THE LOCKER ROOM)!

AS WOMEN TOGETHER, LET'S GET THIS
STRAIGHTENED OUT. TALK TO MANAGEMENT AS I
HAVE. IF YOU DON'T WANT TO GET INVOLVED, BE
CAREFUL—THEY ARE WATCHING US!

THANKS, A B

I worked out there every day for a week after I had posted the letter. I
made a difference. The women were shocked and demanded that management replace the door and install a lock. The gym environment really
changed, especially for the women. The notes were up for probably two

days, but that was all it took. Management didn't listen to me, but they did listen to every woman in the club. Even if only ten women saw the note, I knew they had spread the word. I remember being in the locker room getting dressed and hearing the women talking about it. It made me smile inside, knowing I helped make things a little better for women that day.

Chapter 13

ONCE I SETTLED into my new apartment, I decided it was time to find another job. I wanted to pay more than $79 a month, and I wanted to take more classes at the college. I kept my day job at the dry cleaners, but added a part-time evening job working at a casino selling change.

I had only worked at the casino for a few weeks when they decided to have a meeting to discuss all the changes the casino was going though during an expansion.

I was sitting in a large, beautifully arranged room. There were fifteen round tables with burgundy tablecloths. The tables were full, surrounded by other workers and supervisors. There was a serve-yourself refreshment table loaded with donuts, muffins, fruit, soft drinks, coffee, and mineral water. It reminded me of the eight-hour training course we had to attend before we could work at the casino.

The course was mainly to teach everybody about sexual harassment and discrimination. We watched films, did role-playing, and answered questionnaires about different situations. I thought it was great. With such a variety of people working in the same environment, it was an important course and I respected it.

We were given definitions of sexual harassment, sexism, and sex discrimination. We learned how to recognize behaviors that could be defined as sexual harassment; we also learned ways to prevent and stop it.

We learned that sexual harassment is not about sex. It is about power and control. We discussed the difference between flirtation and harassment, and how flirting feels good and harassment feels bad. The different types of harassment were explained—environmental, verbal, physical, visual, and written. We had questions to ask ourselves in evaluating our own behavior. Would I say it in front of my parents? Would I say it or behave in the same way to members of the opposite or same sex? Is there equal power between us? The course offered a lot of good information.

Working there, however, I experienced tons of sexual harassment, and nobody seemed to care. The rules were not enforced, and the bosses did not seem concerned, maybe because they were part of the problem. The worst harassers were the security guards. I would stand and watch everything going on. It was disgusting. Not only were coworkers harassed, but the customers as well. Any woman walking around who appeared attractive was a target. The spotter would point her out to any other security guard or male worker at the casino. The security guards would even go so far as to call to others on their radios warning them to keep their eyes out for "the woman wearing a red sweater and black pants." So they would all be on the lookout for her. I wondered what would happen if she found out this was going on, that people were treating her like this, that she had become a thing, an unknowing player in their game.

I had been working there for about two weeks when they decided to add cigarette sellers to the casino. This position required the women to wear fish net stockings and very short gold shorts. I had talked to most of the women who would be wearing them, and they didn't like it. A couple of them seemed a bit twisted when they said they wanted the men to dress like them, not the other way around. Others liked the idea, because they knew they would get better tips. Most of the women I talked to hated it but needed the money. Period.

The meeting was almost over. I sat at one of the front tables and one of the superiors finally asked, "Any further questions?"

I raised my hand and said, "Yes, I have a question."

"OK, go ahead," he said.

"Why did you have us all take an eight hour course on sexual harassment and then you turn around and promote it with the outfits you want the cigarette women to wear?" I demanded.

He coughed, and looked behind him smirking to one of the other bosses and said, "I haven't even seen the outfits, have you, Don?"

Of course, Don hadn't seen them either. Therefore, they could make no comment about it at that time.

I knew I wouldn't be working there much longer, but I wanted to leave with something for people to think about. A couple of weeks later the outfits were changed.

Chapter 14

AFTER I QUIT the casino, I wanted to find a good fulltime job that would be permanent. I was tired of bouncing from job to job. I needed stability. I also believed it was time to leave the dry cleaners and find something of interest to me. I wasn't brave enough to look for work involving writing, so I found a job selling new and used exercise equipment.

I was new and the only female in the store. The guys I worked with had been there for years. I learned a lot in a short time. They had one approach: only help the pretty women or the people who looked like money. My approach was different. I wanted to help people, especially women.

Whenever an overweight woman walked into the store, I was excited. I imagined her lean and healthy. I approached her with enthusiasm, but not too much. I didn't want to scare her. I asked her what she was looking for in exercise: health or appearance? It was usually both. I wasn't good at sales. I didn't care if I made the sale. I cared if I inspired people to take better care of themselves. Some of the women seemed intimidated by the men I worked with. So was I.

They were cocky and arrogant. After the newness of my working there wore off, the attention they were giving me became negative. Stares, comments, and slaps on the ass, their reach for a pen also meant a skim across my breast. They were all engaged or living with their girlfriends or both. Their friends would come into the store to check me out. I got phone calls from people I'd never seen, "Tom said you're pretty good looking."

It didn't take long before I was feeling bad about myself. I wanted to be treated equally and taken seriously. I didn't want to quit another job. I didn't know what I was doing wrong. And I had nobody to talk to about it.

***

She was feminine and confident, wearing a short blue skirt and a loose-fitting floral print blouse. As soon as I saw her, I thought she might be a lesbian. She was walking around not trying to impress anybody, yet she was, everybody, even me. She intrigued me. Her dark hair and athletic body were similar to my own. But the way she carried herself reminded me of the person I was trying to be.

While I was ringing up her purchase, a set of five-pound dumbbells, our eyes met and my heart started bleeding. I was looking into my spiritual mirror. I was her, and she was me in every way but physically. I wondered if she felt the connection. We exchanged a few words. Then she turned and headed for the door. My heart sank into deep loneliness as she walked away. Suddenly, she turned around and came back toward me. She approached the counter and our eyes met again. We were both nervous. She didn't say anything, and I didn't know what to say.

Finally, "What's your number?" she asked.

"Here, I'll give you my card." I wondered if she wanted it for business or if it was personal.

"Do you work a lot?" she asked.

"I try not to," I said.

She laughed.

"I'm usually here in the evenings."

"OK, I'll call you."

"Please do."

This time when she walked away, my heart was flying with the butterflies.

The assistant manager, Tom, walked over to me and sarcastically asked, "What was that all about?"

Not saying the "Fuck off" I wanted to, I walked away saying nothing.

The next day I went to work full of anticipation, hoping she would call. She did. It was around 8 p.m. I had just helped a customer load a skier into her car. I stopped at the water cooler, grabbed a white cup from the dispenser tube and filled it with water. I started walking toward the phone before it rang. I felt her call coming.

We talked until about eight-thirty, when I started getting busy with customers. I hated to let her go, but I asked her to call back around nine-fifteen. She said she would. The time wouldn't move fast enough. I couldn't wait to hear her voice again, to hear her laugh again. She was so stunning to talk to and so familiar to me. At times, I felt as though I was talking to myself, and it was some sort of odd dream. I never really had a girlfriend like me. I usually hung out with guys or by myself. So when I talked to her I realized I'd missed having a female friend.

"Are you a lesbian?" she asked.

My first thought was she was a lesbian, but I didn't care, I still wanted to be her friend. I liked her. "No, I'm not. Are you?" I asked.

"No, I'm not. I just thought I'd better ask. I was afraid I might have given you the wrong impression. I mean, after all, I did pick you up."

We both started laughing. I told her how I thought maybe she was, but I didn't care; I still wanted to know her. She said she felt the same way, but we both wanted to avoid that uncomfortable situation.

In time I learned Julie felt the same way I did about many issues: religion, sex, relationships, men, cooking, marriage, children, families, money, prejudice, work, art, dancing, sports, everything. She was one of the first women I ever met who was so similar to me. The only true difference was she was a fighter, not fighting other women. She fought for what she believed in, and fought for her rights as a person. Recently, I'd had my moments of fighting back, but I spent many years just going along. I never wanted to come across like a bitch, so I would go with the crowd or I'd shock them with their own attitudes about women, only a hundred times worse. It kept me protected and from dealing with the way I was being treated as a woman.

Over the next few weeks, Julie became my best friend. We spent time together doing all the things we loved. We had so much common ground and we had many similar experiences in life. I learned a lot from her. She was smart, strong, and a blast to be around. She always encouraged me to be stronger, which made my life happier. At times, we couldn't spend enough time together, but when I did need time and space to be alone, so did she. We could go a week without talking, but when we reached each other again, we'd have so much to talk about and share with each other. We both kept moving forward with our goals: music and writing.

Chapter 15

IN THE MONTHS that passed, Julie cut her first CD and began touring local bars. I had written lyrics for one of her songs and had a few short pieces published in local magazines. I quit my job after I was hired to write for a women's newspaper in the city. I had never been happier. I was finally doing what I was on this earth to do.

It was time for me to move. I found a clean small apartment downtown close to where I'd be working. It had venetian blinds, a fireplace and ceiling fans.

It was hard to leave my pink prison cell. Moving there had been my first step to improving my life. It was an emotional day saying goodbye to Tad, who was moving to Montana the next month and getting married. I moved the few things I had worth keeping: a stereo, computer, books, clothes and papers. I was mixing some of my sentimental feelings with fear of change. But I was excited, too.

I bought a bed first and put it in the living room so company would have a place to sit. I would get other things as I could afford them.

Before I started my new job, Julie and I took off on a one-month road trip. It was a vacation for Julie, but I had an ulterior motive. I needed to face some of my demons.

We decided to head west to visit my unknown father. That trip took us to Canmore, AB. We found him in the country where he lived in a trailer on three acres. He had thirteen dogs, including nine little week-old puppies. He had one cat I never saw, three birds that talked, chirped, and whistled all the time, two horses, and a donkey. Two of the dogs had only three legs and, besides the nine puppies, eight dogs were indoor pets. The dogs ran the place. My dad allowed them on the kitchen table so they could look out the window. They sat around us while we ate dinner, and afterwards, the dogs helped with the leftovers and the dishes.

Julie and I shared a room with a private bathroom in the back of the trailer. The first morning I woke to dogs barking. I rubbed my eyes and lifted the blind to look out the window beside my bed. I had forgotten for a moment where I was. When I remembered, I was afraid I had made a mistake coming to see my dad. It had been an emotionally exhausting night for all of us.

I saw the gate door open, and I suddenly became the little girl who missed her daddy all these years. For the first time in my life, I knew what it felt like to have a dad. I saw him coming through the six-foot privacy fence gate carrying a gallon of milk, and I knew it was for me. I had seen friends' dads doing this when I was young, but it always seemed foreign. Now, I had a dad and he was taking care of me, making sure I had milk for my cereal.

I stayed in bed for a while just to soak it all up. I couldn't believe I was in my dad's house. I feared I might be stirring up the past that had been lying dormant for the last 26 years of his life. But does he owe me something? His youngest daughter was in his life for the first time.

I looked around the room. A dirty yellow rain coat hung behind the bedroom door. The closet had two sliding doors off their tracks exposing about a foot on each side. On the right, hung an old marine uniform with a clear plastic garment bag protecting it. The left side was filled with old marine shirts, torn and faded, mixed with some plaid flannel shirts. Next to the closet was a built-in shelf and some drawers. On the shelf were two wooden boxes and one large green tin box with marine stickers plastered all over it. I wanted to look through the boxes. I wanted to look through the drawers. Leaning against the wall stood a rifle and two shotguns. There was a small desk that held a lamp, a telephone that didn't work and three boxes of bullets, two unopened. Julie had put her songbooks on this desk. On the floor was Julie's guitar and open suitcase.

I looked at Julie. She was still sleeping.

Later that morning, Julie took off for the day. Dad and I stayed home. We looked at pictures, slides and went through those boxes from the bedroom. We came to a section in one of the photo albums that he skipped over quickly. I asked him why and turned the pages back to see. They were pictures of my mom when she was younger and several photos of my sisters and me. He quickly got up to leave the room. I said, "Dad, this doesn't still bother you, does it?"

He said, "No," and began to walk away. With his back facing me, he said, "Yes, it still bothers me." He turned to face me and said, "It bothers me a lot." He was crying.

I was stunned. I couldn't decide if this bittersweet feeling was victory. I wanted to know he was hurt for leaving us, to know he had made a mistake, but I didn't want to witness his pain.

He walked out of the room. In some ways, I felt abandoned again. There was a tightening in my chest. I wondered where he was going and why he was leaving me. I didn't hear his truck start, so I decided he was going to get more memories from the garage to share with me. He did. Only they weren't my memories, they were the things I had been told about my father.

He sat down next to me. I could smell the booze on his breath and the smell of pot on him. He was still drinking. I had wanted to ask, but now I didn't have to. Having me there was hard on him. He kept running to his crutch when things got a little tough.

My dad had many slides of his time spent as a Marine. Another memory that sent him to the garage to medicate his pain. I was heartless in asking him questions. I only heard my inconsiderate self after I saw his response, his quick reflex to get away from me. I couldn't understand his reaction; it was so long ago. I asked him if he killed people. He stood, again with his back facing me; he said that he had. He assured me he was done talking about it. He would not be answering another question from me. And he headed to the garage.

My dad and I went for drives around town. We talked about his life; he showed me places where he had done rockwork, and he took me to a tourist town named Three Sisters. I believe he lived right next to Three Sisters because of his three daughters. Dad and I walked around the shops for a couple hours. He bought me an ice cream cone in a small shop where I confided in him that I wanted to be a writer.

"Somebody in this family has to make it as a writer," he said as if he already knew it would be me.

"What makes you say that?" I asked.

"Well, my mom wanted to be a writer, both my brothers were writers... but nobody really put in the effort to make it happen."

I was inspired. I never knew these people, but I was suddenly connected to this other half of me. My heart so desperately wanted it to be me and not just for me but for them, too. "Maybe it's me. Maybe I'll be the one to make it."

"That's what I think."

God, I love my dad.

I bought a sterling silver ring so I would never forget my dad, that town and my trip to see him.

The last morning Julie and I were there, Dad was going to the gas station to fill his truck with gas and asked me if I wanted to go along. When we got there I became his little girl again, and I was happy to be with my daddy. I'm not sure if it was because he was also buying beer, but he seemed happy to have me with him and told me to pick out a treat. That's when I heard him tell the attendants that I was his daughter. He spoke with such pride. I put my licorice on the counter and heard him ask for ten dollars in lottery tickets.

While we were at my dad's, Julie left us alone as much as possible. I knew this whole experience was hard on her. She hadn't seen her father in fifteen years, and last year found out he had died of alcoholism. She had unanswered questions herself. Every night before bed I would tell her what I learned about my dad. My dad became her dad, and she was making peace, as I was.

The day we were leaving, my dad begged me to stay. "Please just one more day."

"We really need to keep moving. We have others to see."

"I bought lottery tickets. I might win; just wait until after tomorrow. The drawing is tonight. If I win, I'll buy you a big RV so your trip will be nicer. I think I might win. If I win, I'll buy you anything you want. I didn't get to give you anything. Let me buy you something if I win the lottery."

"No, Dad. We have to go."

Julie shook my dad's hand, then gave him a hug. She waited in the car while Dad and I said our goodbyes.

I was nervous about our goodbye. I felt guilty for leaving. I knew how badly he wanted us to stay. I believe he thought with me there he would surely win the lottery and he would be able to get rid of some of his own guilt if he could buy me something. The last few days piled up on me as I was walking toward the hug goodbye. My throat was tight, my eyes burning fighting the tears. I didn't want him to see me like this; I did not want him to hurt any more than he already did. I didn't want him to know how hurt I was. I wanted him to believe I was fine, that I didn't need him. I did need him. I needed to understand him. And I did.

It was the best hug I'd ever had in my life. It was the hug I wanted from every man I'd ever dated. It was the hug I had been missing in my life. I never felt so loved, so connected to another human being. My dad wouldn't let me go, and I held on just as tight. I finally had him. How could I let him go? We stood holding, healing each other through our tears and each other's desire *not* to let go.

Chapter 16

DRIVING AWAY MADE me cry until I fell asleep. Julie knew it would be hard on me, so she drove. All my life I believed we were too much trouble. That he left me because he wanted to find a better life without me. I realized he was just running from his demons just like I had been. Trying to survive the chase, burying everything that came along that hurt. Not wanting to allow the pain to surface, not wanting to expose it to the world, a world we believe hurt us in the first place.

When I woke, I couldn't cry anymore. My dad was gone. I was with Julie, and I wasn't that little girl anymore.

When Julie noticed I was awake, she reached over and put her hand on my thigh. "You OK?"

"Yeah. Thanks." I put my hand on hers and gave it a squeeze. I reached to the sun visor and pulled it down. I flipped the mirror open and looked at myself. My eyes were swollen and red. "Wow," I said with a giggle.

Julie looked over and giggled, too. "It was a rough one."

"Yep, but a good one."

"Yep."

We finally got past Missoula, Montana, and headed toward the Seeley Lake area where Tad was getting married. We were hot and sweaty from driving, so we found a lake along the way to bath in. Nobody was around so we decided to skinny dip in the freezing water. Julie threw her suit on the beach first. It took me a little longer to be sure it was safe. We laughed at each other as we scrubbed our armpits with our hands. I laughed harder when Julie informed me she was cleaning out her butt. I couldn't see what she was doing but her movements supported her statement. I decided to clean mine, too. We didn't want to pollute with soap so we didn't use any. We shampooed our hair and scrubbed our pits and butts with lake water.

Julie didn't care to look around before she got out of the water. From the water I watched her dry off as a man and his daughter walked by. We all ignored each other. Once they were out of sight, I ran out of the water grabbed my towel and suit and ran to the car. Julie stayed behind to dry off in the limited sunlight coming through the trees.

Once safely out of sight in my car, I began to get ready for the wedding. I reached in back for the lotion. The pump on the bottle was stuck. I turned the bottle around and noticed it was Jergen's hand lotion. I paused in the memory of a childhood dream.

Julie knocked on the passengers window and opened the door, "You OK?" she asked getting in the car. "You look like you've seen a ghost."

"Yeah, I'm fine. I just remembered something about my dad. See this lotion?" I asked, showing her the bottle.

"Oh, yeah, it sticks sometimes," she said reaching for it.

"No. It's Jergen's. That's my dad's name. I used to romanticize that this was my dad's company. I only used Jergen's products for years because it made me feel close to my dad."

"Wow. That's kind of cool."

"I knew one magical day he'd find me and tell me that Jergen's was his company. I would tell him, I already knew, and that I only used Jergen's. I thought that would make him proud."

"I wish it was his company," Julie said. "You know what I used to do? I found a man's shirt in the basement when I was young. I made up my mind that it had been my father's. I never asked my mom because I didn't want to ruin the fantasy," she said with a smirk on her face. "Anyway, I kept that shirt under my pillow every night, and I would pray to God, who I just happened to believe *was* my dad, that he would come and find me and want to live with me and Mom."

"Well, what happened to the shirt?"

"Well, I started giving ultimatums to God. Please come back to me by Christmas, by Easter, by Mother's Day… Dad never came back so I burned his shirt. Unfortunately, I burned down the garage, too."

"What! You're kidding?"

"No. I'm not kidding. It was a long time ago, and I still think God was punishing me for giving the ultimatum."

We sat in silence and finished getting dressed and ready for the wedding.

We held hands laughing as we walked up to the bed and breakfast resort where the ceremony would take place. I felt natural and earthy and special next to all the nicely dressed guests who just came from their hotel room showers.

We stayed long enough to congratulate Tad and his new wife, meet some of their family and friends, and have some cake and punch.

Chapter 17

WE FOUND A place to camp by a lake, about a hundred miles out from Evergreen. We set up camp and cooked our veggie dogs over the fire. After dinner, it was too dark to write, so we sat up for a few hours and talked about my father and my only real memory of him.

I was at my grandparent's house with my mother and two older sisters. It was summer, which didn't mean a lot to me since I wasn't in school yet. Besides my family, there was also a strange dark-haired man, a man said to be my father, whatever that meant. I'd heard the word before, but I was not sure how it related to me. My mom and sisters were all I'd ever had. Now this man was going to take my sisters and me on a picnic in my grandparent's pasture.

He pulled the green backpack onto his back, and we walked out the door. Suddenly, he whisked me up and set me on his shoulders. I knew I was supposed to be happy, so I was. My sisters and I were quiet with this stranger. We walked down the graveled road. He was singing and yodeling, holding hands with my sisters, one on each side.

At the picnic site he spread out a blanket and started to set up for the meal. We watched him start his small portable camping stove. We three little girls, in bright clothes and ponytails, sat on the blanket with our legs crossed.

We were finishing up the meal when a spider crawled onto the blanket. I was startled and moved closer to my sister, Debbie, keeping my eyes on the spider. It was big and a color of silver I'd never seen on a spider before and never since. All three of us were scared and tried to get away from the monstrous bug.

This man calmly and compassionately said, "Oh, you don't have to be afraid. Do you know what kind of spider that is?"

"No," we said kneeling quietly, watching.

"Well, that's a Thump Spider," he said, as he flicked his finger at the spider and sent it flying through the air into the weeds of the pasture.

We all laughed in relief. At that moment, the stranger became my dad, my hero. I liked him, and I wanted him around forever.

That was the last time I ever saw my daddy. I always felt like a part of me had been missing all these years. I was like a little girl wandering around, alone in this huge world, searching for that missing part. I turned over rocks, looked behind trees, not knowing what I was looking for, but still always looking.

He abandoned me; he left me alone to face the world. I never got a chance to know him. I wanted a father.

Years later, I learned what my mother went through during this visit from my father. She had gone alone to pick him up at the bus station. With her hair and makeup perfect, and wearing nice clothes, she anxiously awaited his arrival. Her hopes were high that he would again be the man she married, and when they saw each other, they would fall in love a second time.

Her let down came as soon as he stepped off the bus. He looked run down with long hair and dirty clothes. The first words from his mouth were insults followed by the stench of alcohol. Though it hurt, she wasn't ready to give up. There was still a chance that when he saw how special his three little girls were, he would want his family back again.

While we were on our picnic with my father, my mother was with my grandparents, afraid she would never see us again. She thought he might take us. Her fears led to tears, so my grandfather started driving out on the graveled road past the pasture every twenty minutes or so to be sure we were still there and OK.

When I heard my mother's side of this day, my father became unimportant compared to her. Though she had her struggles, she didn't abandon us. She stayed with us and raised us by herself. She is the one who would have thumped the many scary spiders throughout my life if she hadn't been afraid of them herself.

Chapter 18

ON OUR WAY to Colorado, we stopped off at lakes along the way. It was hot, and I didn't have air conditioning in my car, so we'd get out the air mattress, pump it up and lie out for a couple hours on the lake. It was on one muddy lake somewhere in Wyoming that I realized I was making the best memories of my life on this trip. We were a team. Neither of us was better than the other. I didn't feel like I had to look pretty. I didn't have to question whether or not she thought I was acting stupid. We both did at times. We asked each other for help, without feeling rescued. We were friends, best friends.

I lay on the air mattress on my stomach. Julie lay next to me on her back. She was reading a magazine from back to front like she always does. I wondered if having my toes in the water would attract fish, especially with my toe rings on. I dipped my fingers into the cool muddy water and pulled them back out. My ring was shinning in the sunlight. It looked to be a high quality diamond. Though small, it let off a brilliant sparkle. Sadness came over me and I couldn't control it. I began to sniffle without realizing. Memories of my grandma flooded over me, grabbed a hold of me and I couldn't back out. My eyes blurred.

"You know, Julie, I always wanted my grandma to be proud of me, but she wasn't. She always had to worry about me," I said, then thought about how Grandma and I had a secret understanding after her first stroke. She was one of my life teachers. The few words she spoke to me always made an impact.

I remember sitting at the kitchen table alone. My whole family was in the living room talking. She came over to me, sat down and said, "Don't forget you have family who loves you."

"I know, Grandma. I'm fine," I said trying to be cute. But we both knew I was making bad decisions.

She kept staring into my eyes.

"What, Grandma?"

"Don't go to the street."

"Grandma, I would never."

But in some ways, I already had and she probably knew it.

"Angie, I'm sure your grandma was proud of you." Julie said.

"See this ring?" I took it off my finger and handed it to her. "It belonged to my grandma. I found it imbedded in their dirt driveway when I was five, and I gave it to her. She cleaned it off and kept it for weeks, asking neighbors and family if they had lost a ring. After a month passed, my grandma began wearing it for special occasions. Her wedding ring had a very small diamond, and she often wore the one I gave her instead of the one Grandpa gave her. I liked to think it was because I had given it to her, but it might have been the bigger diamond." I grinned and took the ring back from Julie.

"I always wanted to be a success for her. I wanted to buy her a huge diamond ring, four times the size of this one."

Julie watched me slide it back on my finger.

"I think my grandma had big dreams but ended up living as a farmer's wife raising kids. I always hoped one day she could live through me."

"You *are* her huge diamond. Maybe you were a diamond in the rough back then, but you *are* a diamond now."

"You're way too nice to me!" I smiled. "At my grandma's funeral, after her second stroke that took her life, an old woman approached me and asked me who I was. I told her. She firmly grabbed my hand and sat down next to me. I asked her who she was, and she began to cry. 'I was in your grandmother's stroke support group.' she said. 'Oh, that group meant so much to my grandma,' I told her.

I remembered how the stroke group was the one safe place for my grandma to be after she suffered her first stoke ten years earlier. She was closer to those people than she was her own family at times. They understood why she had a hard time speaking. They understood why her movements were slower. Grandma asked me to go with her once. I didn't go. I wish I had.

"She went on to tell me that she was the only one left out of the six who started the group. All the others had had their second or third stroke which took their lives. I sensed her fear that she was next and that maybe being with me brought her closer to my grandma's life; it brought me closer to my grandma. I felt for her, and I stayed with her while she was there. She held onto my hands as if she wanted me to save her. I hoped my grandma was watching and was proud of me for taking care of her friend."

I saw Julie wipe her eyes.

"Will you fuckin' stop!" Julie yelled and jumped off the float. She held her breath and went under the water.

I thought she was kidding or that I had made her sad, too. I didn't understand.

When she came back up, she pushed her hair back from her face. She wasn't smiling. She was angry. "Don't you fuckin' get it? God! Stop fuckin' talking and fuckin' write it! Don't you know why you have such strong feelings? Why you're so sensitive? You are the most talented writer I've ever read! You write the stuff I want to read—the stuff that matters. God keeps giving you reasons to write—things to write about and you're going to fuckin' blow it! I haven't seen you write one thing since we left your dad's. You can't tell your stories as good as you can write 'em! Fuckin' get off the mattress! We're going to get you some notebooks, because you've obviously run out of paper. There is no other reason you would stop writing!"

I got off the mattress, but I swam out toward the middle of the lake. No motorized boats were allowed on the lake, so I wasn't worried about getting hurt. I'm a good swimmer and my anger kept me moving. Once I stopped swimming, I treaded water long enough to realize she was right. I had stopped writing during a time when I could be creating my best work. I swam back to shore.

"You were a bitch to me. And you know how I hate that word."

"I know," she said. "But I needed to say it. I guess I wanted to give you a jolt."

"You did." I was no longer angry.

She walked over to me and we hugged. "While you were in the middle of the lake, I dug your notebooks out of your bag."

I smiled.

"You know, Angie, what just went on out there really had nothing to do with you." She paused. "If I put my music down for a day, I panic inside that I've lost it. So when you stopped I became panicky that you might quit, I might lose you... this thing we've started."

"You're not going to lose me. And I am not going to quit writing." I backed up to break our hug and face her. I held her hand in mine. "I guess right now I'm doing some soul searching... facing my demons."

Chapter 19

WE WERE IN Colorado for four days, I to see my mom and Julie to see an aunt and uncle, so we parted ways.

Before the trip, I had been reading a book on overcoming childhood sexual abuse. The question to confront or not to confront the abuser had been heavy on my mind. On some days, I fantasized facing him; other's, I felt so good about myself I thought what would be the point of putting myself through it. I knew the threat of another assault, not of my body but of a much deeper part of me. He could deny it ever happened.

***

It was early morning. The room was just beginning to lighten, and I was beginning to waken in the chill of the morning air. I was snug under the covers wearing my favorite pajamas, a green and white horizontal striped T-shirt. Ben crawled in bed with me while I was waking. He shouldn't have been there with me and I was scared. I was too afraid to move. I was frozen. His arm reached for me. Oh, God, why? He pulled me close to him. His other arm wrapped around me from underneath to keep me from getting away. His breathing was getting heavier and faster, and his hand was rubbing up and down my thigh. His hand moved to the crotch of my panties, and he slid his fingers under them.

"You're a big girl. You're so beautiful. I'm falling in love with you. Don't tell anyone OK? It will be our secret," he said between moans.

I did not cry. I didn't scream. I didn't yell. I did not tell him to stop. I lay there and let a grown man finger me. His finger cut into me like a knife. He tore my skin. He made me bleed. He hurt me. Me! Eleven-year-old me! WHY?

Remembering that day felt different to me now. A shift had taken place. I remembered something else that happened that day.

That was the day I started believing in angels.

That man had a hold on me that couldn't be broken, until my angel walked in. The door flew open as if the wind was pushing it or someone had barged in. Nobody was there, but he jumped, broke his hold on me, and slid as far over to the other side of the bed as he could without falling out. It gave me just enough time to run down the hall into the bathroom, and lock the door.

I remember when I was younger, I thought evil wanted me and used to fight with my angel. It scared me. It usually happened when I went to bed at night, lying in the dark. My eyes were shut, but I wasn't sleeping. I had to wait for the fight to be over before I could fall asleep, too much commotion. Everything went from one extreme to the other. I'd be lying there, so heavy and weighted down it was impossible to move. Then, suddenly I was so light that if I moved, I'd surely float to the ceiling.

I never talked about my angels, and I never talked about being molested. The wars continued within me, fading, but never truly going away.

When Ben came over, I stayed in my room. I listened through the wall to the talking and laughter between my mother, sisters, and him. My mom would holler to me, "Angie. Come out here. Ben's here to visit." I would ignore her. I was angry and afraid that I was the only one who knew who this man was, and I hoped above all that my sisters didn't know.

His visits came less and less often, and finally stopped. I was able to bury what had happened to me. It wasn't until I was a senior in high school it surfaced again. I went to talk to one of my favorite teachers one day after school. He taught psychology, and I felt safe around him. He had gray eyes that matched his hair.

I didn't feel that I was like most of the girls I went to school with. They were dating or had steady boyfriends; most were even having sex. I didn't want to date, I didn't want a boyfriend, and I certainly didn't want to have sex. I was the only virgin among my friends, and I wondered why. I was attractive enough. Many of the boys did show interest in me. I didn't understand why being around boys was such a problem for me.

I explained this to my teacher and with his first question, the old wound was wide open again. "Were you molested when you were younger?" he gently asked.

Then, I didn't know what to call it. Now, I knew what it was, and I knew I had been. I became hot with hurt boiling over within me. After a long silence, "Yes," I said.

He continued, "I'm going to ask you a question with a choice, and I want you to pick one. OK?"

"OK."

He spoke slowly with concern in his eyes. "Angie. One, is over the clothes. Two, is under the clothes. Three, is intercourse. Can you tell me which number it was?"

"It was two."

"Angie, I'm going to tell you something and you need to believe this." He looked right into my eyes and said, "It was not your fault."

With those words, I started to cry. How did he know? He wasn't there. "OK."

I had found Ben's phone number and address about a month before our trip, just in case I decided to confront him. I didn't tell Julie my plans because I knew she would insist on going with me and I didn't want pressure to do something I wasn't sure I wanted to do. I was also a little concerned she might attack him and that wasn't my intention. Besides, then I was a child and alone; now I needed him to know I'm strong, strong enough to do this alone.

I drove to his house, not sure what I would do. I was shocked to find that he lived in the same place. I sat in my car in front of his house and waited. My heart raced every time I reached for the door handle to go in, and I would stop. Why did he get to go on living, and I had to be in a prison all these years—a prison of fear, paralysis, and suspicion. I punished myself day after day, week after week, year after year.

He came outside and I watched him mow his small front yard.

I remembered everything about his house and everything about that day. I remember him making us spaghetti after it happened. He stood at the stove and stirred the sauce like it was a normal day. It would never be a normal day again for me. He bumped his head on the hood above the stove. I remember that. I remember the pain of his knifelike finger cutting me. I will always remember that pain. I remember how long I stayed in the shower that day. I remember how my tears mixed with the water, and my moaning was hidden in the crash of the water hitting my skin and the tub and the walls of the shower. I remember how the tub was slightly higher than the floor and as I got out of the tub I thought I would fall, the floor wasn't where I expected it to be. I started reaching for the wall and the towel bar in front of me to catch my fall and then there it was, the floor. I didn't fall that day.

I remember his arms around me, the same arms I felt years later in men I dated. Those arms wrapped around me still hurt, still remind me. I still cry for that eleven-year-old little girl.

I wasn't sure what I was looking for or what I needed him to do. I'm not sure why I would think this man who hurt me so badly would be the same man who could save the rest of my life, but in some twisted way that's what I believed.

I faced him that day. I sat with him for three hours but, more importantly, I sat with myself. I went through all the emotions and memories that eleven-year-old girl had. The best gift I could have given her, I gave. She didn't want to go in. And I didn't make her. I sat with her in the car and let her confront him in her own way. It wasn't about the adult me; it was about her; it happened to her, not to me.

The next day the adult me had to make it clear to the little-girl me that what he did was very wrong. I called the police to find out the statute of limitations. I wanted to file a report. I was put on hold several times before they connected me to the right person. A man answered. I had expected a woman.

"How old was the victim?" he asked.

"Eleven."

"How long ago did it happen?"

"A long time ago."

"Ten years is the statute of limitations," he stated.

"OK."

"Has it been too long?" he asked.

"Yes, it has."

"Sorry." He was sincere.

"That's OK," I said because I had a plan B.

I grabbed my laptop and wrote a letter to the police. I put all the facts and all the information in the letter. I put his full name, address and telephone number. I stated that he sexually abused an eleven-year-old girl in the summer of 1984. I told what happened in detail. I also stated that I knew the statute of limitations had expired but I needed to make a report anyway. I thanked them for their time and signed my full name.

I went to the library to use their printer. I bought a stamp and envelope and mailed it off that day. It felt great. I let it go. It was out of my hands.

Chapter 20

THE NEXT MORNING I left the house early before my mother was up. It was still dark. I went to the gas station down the road and grabbed a French vanilla latte from their machine. I filled my large cup only half full so I wouldn't spill it while I drove around. Plus, I didn't like to have too much caffeine. The counter woman looked anxious for her shift to be over. I paid and left. My car seemed to drive itself to my destination—Diana's house.

I couldn't stop thinking about a poem I wrote, repeating it over and over again in my mind.

> WHAT HAPPENED TO YOUR FAMILY LIFE.
> WHAT ABOUT YOUR HUSBAND, WHAT ABOUT
>   YOUR WIFE?
> AND THE CHILDREN, THE SWEET INNOCENT
>   KIDS
> WHO NEED YOUR PROTECTION IN ORDER TO
>   LIVE.
> WHO'S GOING TO PROTECT THEM FROM YOU?
> AND THE THINGS YOU SAY AND DO.
> THEY HEAR IT, THEY FEEL IT, THEY LIVE IT.
> THE HATE AND SCREAMING FIGHTS.
> THEY'RE CRYING THEMSELVES TO SLEEP AT
>   NIGHT.

LIVE BY EXAMPLE. WHAT ARE YOU TEACHING
   YOUR BABIES,
TO HATE INSTEAD OF LOVE?
THE FIRES OF HELL OR HEAVEN ABOVE?
IF THEY CAN'T DEPEND ON YOU, THEN WHO?
WHO?

The poem brought back the memory. My mother was out with friends and my oldest sister, Cathy, was babysitting me. A friend of mine called and wanted to know if I wanted to spend the night with her and two other friends. She was having a slumber party. Her mother was not home, but she was sure it would be OK. My sister, who didn't want to be watching me in the first place, said it was OK only if they came and picked me up. It was already dark outside, and Cathy didn't want to have to get me there. They said they'd be right over.

We walked the streets to Sandy's house and played outside until her mother came home. She was drunk and said only one girl could spend the night. Since Tara and I were invited without approval, we were the two to leave. It must have been around eleven o'clock at night, and I was scared. I knew I couldn't go home. If I did, my mother would never let me spend time with my friends again.

So it was Tara and I, alone. She said it would be OK if we stayed at her house. She said her mother wouldn't care. So that's where we headed. I seemed so sheltered compared to her. She knew the streets as if it weren't the first time she had been out, alone, late at night. We were cold and had to ditch cops on the way because of the curfew. We stopped to warm up at the ATM tellers that were open all night.

The walk was only a couple of miles, but it seemed like it took hours to get to her house. When we arrived, her mother, Diana, was also just getting home. Tara, with her short brown hair and tan skin didn't look like her mother who had fair skin and blond hair. When we stepped inside from the cold crisp night, the warmth welcomed me. The house was old, a bit run down, but homey.

Diana seemed happy to have us there. She made us a cookie sheet full of tater tots and French-fries. I thought she was one of the kindest women

I had ever met. She wasn't even mad at Tara for having a friend over or for coming in late at night. Tara told her the truth, and she accepted it. It was nice.

Five minutes after the food was ready, we were all sitting at the large table in the center of the kitchen getting ready to eat. We were hungry. Suddenly someone was at the front door yelling. It was Tara's mom's boyfriend. He was not a large man, but his booming anger scared me. He walked into the kitchen where we were and started throwing things around, screaming at Tara and Diana. I remember him picking up the hot cookie sheet, still full of tater tots and French fries, saying, "Who do you think I am? I don't feed the whole goddamn neighborhood!" And he threw the tray toward Tara and me. We ducked under the kitchen table.

Diana yelled for us to go upstairs to stay until she called us down. The upstairs was small and seemed more like a finished attic with its slanted walls. Diana stayed downstairs, and he beat her.

I sat on the mattress on the floor where Tara slept at night. It was right next to the stairway, and we could hear everything so clearly. Each time he hit her, I felt a deeper numbness. Tara was crying, standing at the top of the stairs. She would walk part way down, change her mind, and walk back up. This went on for about a half an hour until Tara'd had enough. She went straight downstairs, sneaked into the kitchen and called the police.

When Tara said, "Please hurry!" into the phone, Dan looked up and saw she had called the police, but it was too late to take the phone away from her. They were on their way.

Tara ran back upstairs and Dan went straight to Diana. He was yelling at her, threatening her. "If I spend any time in jail over this you're going to be sorry, both of you!" He headed for the door. It slammed behind him and Diana called us down to see if we were OK. We came downstairs and Tara headed outside.

Diana was hurt, physically and emotionally. Her face was swollen and her movements slow. She and I headed outside behind Tara. By the door was a clump of Diana's long blond hair. She looked at it and reached for her head. When she brought her hand back down, it was covered with blood.

The police were pulling up just as Dan was speeding away. Tara ran up to the police car and pointed, "That's him! Go get him!" They caught him around the corner.

Diana was too weak and upset to be strong. She just stood there hugging me, crying, "I'm so sorry, I'm so sorry, Angie."

It was OK. I was just glad she was OK.

The police told Diana to find a safe place to go because they wouldn't be able to keep Dan after about four o'clock in the morning. Diana spent the next few hours on the phone trying to find somewhere to go where Dan wouldn't find us, someplace where we would be safe. I quietly sat in the kitchen with them looking at the mess Dan had made. The walls, floor, and ceiling were covered with broken eggs, ketchup, flour, and milk. The tater tots and French fries were still lying on the floor. At that time, there was no place to go or support women could get. And with each, "No, I'm sorry, you can't come here," came more nervousness and panic. She knew her time was running out. We knew at four o'clock we were going to have to leave, and that's what we did.

Tara was angry at Diana for wanting to stay and work things out. Tara and I left. We went straight to a twenty-four-hour convenience store. She stole a large bag of Reese's Pieces and bought a pack of cigarettes. She said they were for her mom. The cashier hardly spoke and wouldn't have cared if they were for us. We headed over to a railroad bridge. We climbed under the bridge and sat above the river and under the tracks. We smoked and ate Reese's Pieces while our feet dangled toward to water. We acted out the coolest ways to hold a cigarette. I remember getting smoke in my eyes from my own cigarette and her laughing at me. The pain watered my eyes sending tears down my cheeks.

She asked me what I would do if a train came. The thought horrified me. "Would you jump or stay?" she asked.

I didn't know. But after she asked, I didn't want to be there anymore. She laughed at my cowardice and assured me that if a train came we would know it in plenty of time to get out from under the tracks without having to jump.

We stayed there until Tara felt it would be safe to go home. It must have been around seven or eight in the morning when we decided to head back to the house. We weren't far from it, but we had been gone for at least three hours. In the daylight, I could see the rundown neighborhood and the houses needing paint. Tara's was one of them. She had no grass in the front yard, only dirt.

When we got back, Dan and Diana were sleeping, lying next to each other in the living room where he had beaten her just seven hours earlier. Tara and I left again. This time she decided to walk me home, then go back, and deal with her family alone.

Tara was one year younger than I was, yet she had to grow up so fast. She always seemed so much older and wiser. That night and into the morning we really didn't talk much about what happened. I think we both tried to put it behind us. I think now we should have talked about it.

The months of our friendship continued. She taught me things, bad things. We broke into and vandalized schools. I watched her steal everything from jewelry to candy bars. We used each other to stay out all night. She'd say she was staying at my house, and I'd say I was staying at hers. My mom never really knew the truth because I never let my mom get close enough to Tara to figure out the kind of troubled life she lived. We smoked cigarettes all the time and always in the same spot, under the tracks, by a closed-down granary, down a dead-end street.

It was fall, almost winter; everything was gray and cold. Tara and I drifted apart. I heard rumors about her as time went on, and I always knew why. I was too afraid to be her friend.

I drove to the bridge we sat under. It made me sad to think a twelve-year-old had to live that kind of life. Why did Diana allow this to happen? Why did she make Tara grow up so fast? Why at seven in the morning was Dan holding Diana in his arms, while Tara was outside smoking cigarettes under the bridge on a cold fall morning afraid her mother would be killed?

Chapter 21

I DROVE TO the last place I lived with Stan. The sun was beginning to come up, and the slight breeze sprinkled the air with wind chimes. The trees danced. The wind was carrying my angels to me. I started remembering. But it was surreal, as though it hadn't been my life at all, somebody else's. Or maybe, mine but from a hundred years ago.

The house needed painting. It was the same yellowish tan with teal green trim, the same color Stan painted it when we lived there together. It looked run down and old, and that matched my memories of life with Stan.

***

I never dreamed I'd be in a situation like Diana's, but there I was. Almost ten years after I watched Diana frantically searching for a safe place to go, I sat at a table, safe, in a women's shelter. The difference was I had a place to go.

Stan and I had met at the local gym. He was a big man, he had played college football and continued lifting weights after graduation. He was a few years older than my eighteen. We dated, and then married just over a year-and-a-half later. He had been my best friend before the marriage. After, he became my owner. He even had his name on me. The moment we walked back up the aisle, the change had taken place.

The months ahead were full of pain and confusion for me. I did not understand what marriage was all about. I felt lied to, tricked. I thought marriage was something everybody hoped for. This is that one thing I dreamed about my whole life? It didn't register that I may have been with the wrong man, I was afraid every man was the wrong man. The whole thing was a scam, a way to hook and trap women to keep them in their place—a legal way for a man to own a woman and be in control of her.

One night after a fight Stan left. He said he was going to kill himself. I picked up the phone and called a suicide hot line. The man I talked to asked me questions about my relationship with Stan. When I realized what was being said to me, I became even more confused. He was telling me I was being abused. I argued for Stan's sake, "He doesn't mean to hit me. He's going through some hard times. He really does want to kill himself, and I'm afraid it's my fault."

I felt the counselor didn't understand what I was trying to say to him. He just kept telling me I was being abused and Stan needed help. He told me to leave him for my own safety. I felt I knew Stan better than this man, so I continued to stick up for him. I wanted to help Stan. I wanted to be a better wife so Stan wouldn't want to commit suicide anymore. I didn't want to hear it might be a good idea for me to leave my husband. I loved Stan.

But after talking to the counselor for a while, I realized Stan's suicide threats were always directed toward me. I was the one who was going crazy because of the threats.

Stan was sitting on the edge of our king-sized bed with a loaded gun pointed at his head. The safety was off. I sat on the floor at his feet sobbing, trying to get him to put the gun down.

"Please, Stan, don't. I love you! I'm sorry! I'll never leave you. I promise!" I reached over to touch his thigh.

He turned the gun on me. "Get your fuckin' hand off me! It's too late! You did this to me and now you have to pay the price." He turned the gun back to him and cocked it.

"Oh, God, please don't! I love you!"

"No, you don't! You want to leave!"

"No, I don't! I want to be with you! Please put the gun down!"

"Quit crying! It's your fault I'm going to die," he yelled. "I want you to live with this memory for the rest of your life. I'm going to pull the trigger, you'll hear a loud bang and the next thing you'll see will be my blood and brains on that wall. Can you picture it?" he demanded.

"Yes," I cried.

"My dead body will be lying there, and you'll always live with the fact that you killed me. I want you to remember my blood and the pain you caused me!"

After a few hours of this, he'd usually put the gun down and get on the floor with me, holding me in his arms. "Shhhh…everything's going to be OK," he'd say while I cried.

The episodes came often. Sometimes we'd be driving in our car, and he would try to jump out. Usually it was at home, and he'd use either a knife to his throat or the gun to his head. I remember once blacking out and waking up to him trying to get me dressed for work like nothing happened.

The man at the hot line gave me a few other numbers to call because I still had doubts Stan was abusive. I called them. They all told me the same thing, "If you don't leave, your life is in danger." How can they say this to me? I'm married to this man.

The last number I called asked me if anybody knew what I was going through. I had nobody but him. Although my mother lived only a mile away, we never talked. My mother thought Stan was the greatest man on the planet. Anytime I was around her, she would say things like, "I hope one day I find a man like Stan. You're so lucky."

Then there was Stan saying, "Your mom is such a bitch. She's such a fuckin' whore slut. I don't want you around her." So I didn't go around her.

Another way Stan kept me quiet was with stories about his parents' relationship. He told me how they had their problems, but his mother always made it worse because she would run and tell her parents. I believed other family members getting involved could cause problems. He assured me if I told anybody, everything would get worse. I wasn't going to tell. Things were bad enough.

After talking to the counselors from the hotline, I called my mom. She could hear I had been crying, so she came right over. We went for a drive so I could talk openly without the fear of Stan coming home. I unloaded. I told her everything. After crying together she asked, "What are you going to do?"

"I don't know. I guess go to the shelter and talk to someone to start with. But I don't know how I'm going to get away. He always has to know where I am," I said.

"Tell him you're going with me to a volleyball game tomorrow night. Then you can go to the shelter, and he won't be able to find you," she said.

So that's what I did. The shelter knew about my situation because I had called them the same night I called the suicide hot line. They feared if he found out I was getting help, our marriage could end as a murder/suicide. I stopped to call the shelter from a pay phone at a grocery store. The woman who answered the shelter telephone asked me if I had been followed. I said I hadn't. So she gave me the rest of the directions.

Cindy met me at the door. She was naturally pretty with no makeup and her dark hair pulled back. She looked about five years older than I was. She knew a lot more about this than I did. She made room for me at a large table in the middle of the room, moving books and papers from a chair and the table to a filing cabinet. We sat down.

"I have this form I'm going to fill out as I ask you questions," she said. "I want you to just answer yes or no."

The top of the sheet read: ARE YOU ABUSED? HAVE YOU EVER BEEN ABUSED? HAS YOUR INTIMATE PARTNER DONE ANY OF THESE THINGS TO YOU?

"Has he pushed or shoved you?"

"Yes."

"Has he held you to keep you from leaving?"

"Yes."

"Has he slapped or bit you?"

"Yes." And with each yes, she put a check mark by the question.

"Has he kicked or choked you?"

"Well, yes, he's choked me."

She circled choked and put a check by it. "Has he hit or punched you?"

"Yes." By this time, I was feeling very frail and tears were pouring down my face. I never realized how bad it was until I saw it on paper. When I went to the shelter, I really didn't feel I belonged. I didn't realize I was a battered woman.

She asked, "Are you OK?" and got up to get me a box of Kleenex.

"I didn't know it was this bad. I can't believe I'm letting somebody do this to me." It was my first realization about what was happening. And I knew I didn't deserve it; nobody deserved to be treated that way.

"I know," she said. "I'm really sorry. It's hard."

From physical abuse, we went on to the sexual and emotional abuse questions. No question was easy. By the time we were finished there was a check mark beside almost every one. Stan and I didn't have children so those questions were left blank. We moved on. She explained the three phases of battering: the tension building, the explosion and release of tension, and the calm, loving phase. We then went on to myths about battering and the reasons why women stay.

That day I made the decision to leave.

After two and a half years of marriage, I realized I had made Stan more important than myself. I always wanted to make him happy, failing to realize that only he was capable of that. I always thought I could help him through his problems, but he needed to help himself. I also thought things would get better.

They never did. They only got worse.

Chapter 22

I NEEDED SOME time to myself, away from my childhood bed-room full of memories. The moon was bright. I could see the glow of the sky through the window of my hotel room. The street traffic mixed with other sounds. I couldn't decide if it was pipes clanging, people talking or the wind. I was tired but couldn't sleep. I lay in bed thinking about my grandma. I wished she were still with me. I wished I could make some things up to her.

My strongest memory of my grandma came back to me. I rolled over so my back faced the window, and my eyes filled. My warm tear rolled down my slightly chilled face and dropped on to my pillow. I knew I'd never get over the guilt.

***

I traveled from Colorado to Minnesota to be with my grandma during her recovery, leaving my abusive husband behind. In the days I was there, I remember the family trying desperately to find a way to communicate with her. We would ask her questions, then ask her to respond in some way. We wanted her to move a finger if she could understand. We tried asking her to blink once for yes and twice for no. Nothing seemed to work. She couldn't talk, she couldn't move, and so we felt she couldn't understand. But we were wrong.

My husband said if I wasn't on the next bus, he was coming to get me. And of those four days with my grandma, it's the last day that I will never forget.

She was in her room sitting in a chair while I brushed her hair. The family left me alone to say goodbye. While I stood there talking to her back, I wept. I felt safe, knowing that she couldn't understand so I told her how bad it was for me at home. I told her how I wanted to stay with her, but I couldn't because Stan would come and get me. I told her how I was afraid of him and how mean he was to me.

Before I finished brushing her hair I calmed myself down and wiped my eyes. I walked around to the front of her to give her a hug and a kiss good-bye. My heart dropped when I saw her red tear-filled eyes. She had been crying the whole time. My head filled with heat and I tried to deny that she understood. As I hugged her, my cheek touched her wet cheek. No words were needed. *She* understood.

I couldn't forgive myself or face her after that because I was too ashamed. Not only did I have to go back to him and his treatment, I had to live with the guilt of my cruelty. I used her, took advantage of her. I did this to my grandma, who had just suffered a severe stroke. How could I have done that to her?

I drifted off to sleep with my grandma close to me. I loved her so much.

Chapter 23

I MET JULIE at Taco Bell for lunch and found myself telling her my Taco Bell story.

It was the day after my thirteenth birthday. I was proud to be a teenager. I wondered what it meant, how my life would change. I waited in the car while my mom ran into Taco Bell to get lunch. It was a warm spring day, so our windows were down. I was watching and listening to the traffic of people wanting to use the drive-thru window. Cars were coming from the main road and from the alley behind Taco Bell. In time, I realized running in hadn't been any quicker. Mom was still inside and the drive-up window had emptied. I watched the last car pull around and out of sight.

I saw an older red pickup pull into the alley and park behind the used car lot next to Taco Bell. I watched a gray-haired man in his late forties get out and walk over to a young tree next to some garbage cans. He turned his back to me. I assumed he had to go to the bathroom badly. He was wearing faded blue jeans and a blue denim shirt. I kept watching. I could see his arm moving, while his other hand reached up and grabbed one of the branches. Suddenly he turned around and faced me. He was exposed and masturbating. I turned my head in disbelief and looked again to be sure. The windows being down scared me.

My mom walked to the passenger's side to hand me the food. I took it and said timidly, "Mom, that man over there is touching himself."

"Oh, he is not," she said and looked in that direction. "My God!" She rushed around the car and jumped in, driving the wrong way down the one-way alley to avoid passing him.

My mother was laughing nervously in disbelief, looking for a cop or a phone to call the police. We pulled onto First Street and a squad car was heading our way. My mom started flashing her lights and waving her hand out the window. The police car pulled over across the street.

"I can't believe I'm going to go and tell this to a man," Mom said. She got out and ran across the street. I watched her lean in, talking to the officer. She stood and pointed toward Taco Bell. The cop took off in a hurry.

My mom ran back across the street, jumped into the car and said, "That cop was a woman. Thank God it was a woman."

"Jesus, Angie, why don't you just take a gun to your head and get it over with. What is it with you? Have you ever thought of just letting it go?" Julie said.

"I don't think I'm supposed to, not yet."

"You mean you need to write about it?"

"Yes. Sometimes I think I go through it for that very reason. Once it's written, I'll let it go."

"Fair enough." Julie said. "But, maybe you could start integrating some of the good in your life."

"Don't you see the good in this?"

She gave me a questioning look.

"The cop was a woman."

Chapter 24

WHILE I WAS in Colorado, I spent most of my time alone working on my past. But Mom and I got a few opportunities to talk.

I was going to take a shower. Mom yells, "Be careful of Mr. Shetland," and laughs.

I stormed back at her. "What's funny about that?" My mind raced with the memory of growing up living next to Mr. Shetland and the fucked-up messages I got from my mom.

We lived in a corner ranch-style house with two backyard neighbors. Our backyard had a six-foot privacy fence except one small section of chain link fence. That view went straight from Mr. Shetland's heightened backyard straight to our bathroom window.

I was always told by my mother to be careful because he was watching us. As we got older, it became a family joke that wasn't funny to me. She thought it was a riot that he didn't watch her, only her daughters.

I always wondered why she didn't blame him. She held us responsible by instructing us to close the frosted glass window before undressing, cover up with a towel before opening the window to let the steam out. And then make sure to close the shower curtain so he couldn't see us.

"Why didn't you ever put up a privacy fence so Mr. Shetland would stop watching us shower?" I demanded. Before she could answer, I added, "Didn't you care enough about us to protect us? Don't you think a normal shower in our own home that is supposed to be safe would have been good for us?"

"Angie, you're making this into a big deal."

"It is a big deal! Do you know what my showers were like? Hot house, no air conditioner, and opening the frosted glass window meant shutting it as soon as I heard his back door squeak. And how can you still be friends with him? You should hate him for being such a pervert toward your daughters!"

"God, Angie, I didn't know this was such a problem."

"Yeah, you never knew! You never once stopped to think about it. Maybe I was too young and insecure to put my feelings into words back then, but I'm not now!" I looked at her with disgust. "You should have made us important enough to protect us!" I walked out of the house without my shower and went to the gym.

That was all I had to say to her in anger. I was no longer angry, but I was certain guilt was moving in. I knew she had done, just like my father, the best she could. She had her own struggles and problems.

I wondered if it would have been different if there had been a father in our house. Would Dad have walked over to his house and had a talk with him? Would he have built up the fence, or would he have treated the situation the same as my mom?

The only thing I knew for sure was that I didn't feel protected growing up. I questioned if I was protected now as an adult. Or was I too protected? I made it hard for people to get close to me, especially men.

Chapter 25

I SAT OUTSIDE in the courtyard of the gym. From a block away I heard church bells ringing, which reminded me of one of the songs my sister Debbie used to play when she was first taking piano lessons. I could see her sitting at her piano, practicing this song repeatedly, her long brown hair pulled back loosely as her dainty hands pressed the keys. The piano was old and tall, painted white with many coats beneath. There were large flowers in bright pinks, blues, and greens stuck to it, the type of stickers you might find on the bottom of someone's bathtub to keep from slipping.

The memory of my sister made me happy. And I remembered a time when I was lying next to her. Neither of us was sleeping; we were both uncomfortable in a strange bed in a strange room. I could hear my mom talking behind us. She was scared.

Every Father's Day Mom would take us to a hotel. Maybe it was her way of trying to make it up to us for our father not being there. We would play miniature golf, swim, and play video games. It was usually a nice time for all of us. It gave her a chance to relax and get away from her everyday stresses. She was always especially nice to us during this getaway.

Debbie and I were swimming when we noticed a man showing interest in our mother. He resembled my dad; wearing white brought out his tan skin and dark hair. He was checking the chemicals of the pool water.

Debbie and I were yelling, "Mom watch me!" but we were losing her attention to that man. Before long, he was sitting at the poolside table with her, having a drink. They sat together talking the whole time Debbie and I swam. I couldn't help but feel happy, wondering if this would be the one. Would he be my father?

After swimming, Debbie and I got ready for bed while the man and Mom talked. I pranced around the room, trying to be cute so he would want me for a daughter. It was getting late and Mom told him he had to go, but he wanted to stay. He claimed to be drunk and needed to sleep it off for a while. Mom hesitated but didn't want him to get into an accident. She got under the covers and insisted he lay on top of them. Debbie and I were in the next bed with our backs facing them.

His plan was to have sex with my mother. It didn't matter to him that her two young daughters were beside them. He tried all night. I was too afraid to look and Debbie probably wouldn't have let me. She held me tight. She was as scared as I was. I knew he was touching my mom in ways she didn't want him to. He kept her up, he kept my sister up, and he kept me up the whole night through.

Not only did I lose sleep that night, I lost respect for my mother for allowing that to happen, and I lost a part of hope that men are good. I learned that night that men can treat us this way and women have to accept it.

In my fantasy, my mother lets him stay for a while. She then asks him to leave. He refuses. She does not feel obligated to protect him from an accident, she feels obligated to protect her children and herself. She tells him he has to go. Again, he doesn't want to leave. She calmly turns to the phone and dials the front desk. "Will you call the police for me? There is a man in my room with my daughters and me, who won't leave."

She hangs up the phone, turns toward him, and says, "Now what were you saying?"

He says, "OK, I'm leaving!" and he looks around the room for his jacket.

She then sits down on the bed next to Debbie and me, wraps an arm around each of us, saying through body language this man will not fuck with us, and no man will fuck with us.

I wondered if Mom was afraid to face this man. Maybe she had tried to stand up to men in the past and hadn't been able to. Maybe she feared this man beating her up in front of us more than she feared him pawing her all night. Maybe if she had told him he couldn't stay, he would have gotten to the phone before she could make the call. I wondered if she was afraid of men.

I wondered why my mom wasn't stronger. Why didn't she protect me from the pain? Then it hit me. If she couldn't protect herself, there is no way she could have protected me.

I called Julie from the gym and asked her to meet me for dinner in a few hours. She agreed. I knew I'd need her after talking to my mom.

I got in my car and had a hard time getting it into reverse. I was grinding my gears. I knew it was because I was nervous and unsure how I'd talk to my mom. I've never been able to talk to her.

Chapter 26

MOM WAS SITTING in the back yard at the picnic table. I opened the screen door and asked if I could join her. She nodded her head.

I sat down next to her. I didn't want to know, and I couldn't ask. I wondered if somebody hurt her when she was a little girl. I kept my head down. "Please no. Please no," I kept repeating in my mind.

We sat in silence. It wasn't about me anymore. I was in agony that somebody might have hurt my mommy and I wanted to protect *her*.

If she had been hurt, it all made sense. Maybe my mom still had all that poison inside of her, buried, trapped. And she wasn't able to dig it out.

"I'm mad at you sometimes, Mom."

"I know."

"I never really felt safe growing up, and I want somebody to blame." I searched my mind for who I could blame instead of my mother. I was shocked because I hadn't realized it sooner. My body became heavy with the certainty that the blame belonged to my dad for leaving me, Ben for abusing me, that man at the hotel for being a jerk to my mother, Mr. Shetland for watching me shower, and Stan for beating me.

I had blamed my mother for not being stronger. I thought about how I blamed men, all men. I keep that close to me so *they* can't get close to me. It keeps me safe. I don't want another man to hurt me.

"I love you, Mom." I could feel my face crinkle to fight tears, but they came anyway.

My mom reached for me and hugged me. "I love you, too." Her crying became vocal with deep breaths and moans. "I'm sorry I couldn't keep you safe." We held on to each other.

She kept crying and holding onto me and maybe some of the poison was loosening up and seeping out of both of us. I wondered if hearing the words "I love you" from somebody you love back is enough.

Chapter 27

BEFORE I MET Julie for dinner, I went to the bookstore to check out the latest best sellers. Bookstores always inspire me to keep writing. Secretly, I wanted to write a novel. I had many half-written books filed away.

"How are you doing, Julie? Are you having fun with your family?"

"I'm doing OK. I'm not getting a lot of space."

"You're going crazy, aren't you?"

"Let's just say, I'm glad you called. So how are things with your mom?" Julie asked.

I put my fork down and leaned back in my chair. "At times I've been so angry at her." I said. "But I'm beginning to understand some things. I remember JD. Who knows what his real name was. He just went by that because that's what he always drank. He was a serious alcoholic with a big red nose. One guy moved in with us because my mom was over at his house when it started on fire and burned down. I guess she felt obligated. Then there was a guy she called the 'Italian stallion' after the relationship ended. I guess he always wanted to have sex, nothing else, just sex.

"And there was a married truck driver who would take her with him on road trips. Let's see, who else? Darrel, who was not only an alcoholic, but also a gambling addict. A guy by the name of George, who wore plaid shorts, tube socks, and sang a song called Yellow Pages, and those were the only two words in the whole song. I could go on and on," I said with a smirk. "It's really not funny. And what's sad is that I can't say anything about it. I've had my share of creeps."

"It all sounds familiar, Ang," Julie said and took a drink of her water. "And I bet you wanted everyone of them to be your daddy,"

"You got it."

"Now, looking back aren't you glad she didn't settle for one of them? You know, just to get a father for her girls?"

"Yes, but I wish she would have picked better to begin with. It wasn't easy having men in and out of my life."

We sat in silence. The server brought us the dessert menu.

"I remember one guy she really liked; he wanted to marry her. She wouldn't because he was younger and had no children. She thought it wouldn't be fair to him not to have children of his own so she dumped him, even though he said he loved us girls. I remember in the middle of the night, he came over while we were all sleeping. He was drunk and talking crazy about suicide because my mom wouldn't marry him. I remember my mom running next to his pickup, hanging onto the door handle, trying to get him to stop. He just kept on driving away, and he hurt my mom's hand and wrist, almost broke it. She was crying and screaming to him not to kill himself."

"What happened?" she asked.

"I don't know," I said. "I do know I felt bad, I thought the whole thing was my fault. Why weren't we good enough kids for some kind, single man who wanted us? Why was she alone in the first place? Did Dad leave because Mom had me? Was I the straw that broke the camel's back? She always used to say she'd never remarry until we girls were grown. So I always felt it was my fault my mom was alone and lonely. I learned through counseling that young children are very egotistical and think everything is their fault. I know I did. For a long time I believed I didn't deserve to be happy."

"Wow, I think I had the same problem. Thank God we don't have kids to mess up," she grinned.

"I think I was on the path to repeating my mom's lonely, mixed-up life."

"They say it's just a big cycle and we all do it, but I'm going to break this cycle. I'm going to live my own life, with or without a man."

"Yeah, well, about six months after I was married I remember late at night, running next to Stan's pickup, hanging onto his door handle, trying to get him to stop, while he was threatening suicide."

"Talk about a cycle."

"I remember after leaving Stan, I stayed with my sister, her husband and their little girl. I tried to talk to my sister, Cathy, about everything, but she wouldn't listen. She'd just say, 'I don't want to hear a thing about it,' and get up and leave the room. I always felt hurt because I really could have used a friend or just someone to talk to. One day about five years later I drove her and her two little girls to the Dairy Queen. When we were pulling out of the parking lot her oldest daughter asked, 'Mom, do you remember when dad pushed you and you hit your head on the dresser?'"

Shocked, Cathy answered, "Yes. Do you?" and turned to me in concern.

"Why, Cathy? How old was she?" I asked.

"I don't think she was even two."

"It was at that moment I understood why she didn't want to talk to me about my abusive situation with Stan. She was in the same dilemma with her husband."

"Your family is like mine, lots of family secrets, not a lot of talking."

"That's right." I looked up from my angel food cake. "I just wonder if somebody hurt my mom when she was little."

"Maybe," Julie said.

"You know, I'm going to stop blaming my mom. I had an epiphany today. I will blame specific men, who hurt me when I was little, not all men and not my mom."

Julie agreed with a nod and added, "And not yourself."

"My old way of thinking will be hard to change." I put my fork down and pushed my plate away from me. "My mom made her share of mistakes, but I love her. I remember bright clothes she used to sew for us, bright flowers and butterflies in the alley, fun toys, and great friends. Though we were poor, things were good, and that was because of my mom," I said.

"It's never all bad. I guess we have to remember to look at the good occasionally. I mean, could you imagine being your mom, raising three girls with no child support and little family support? Being a divorced woman with kids was not common or easy; isn't easy still, but could you imagine back then? Your mom was a trooper. To top it all off, she's successful. She did it alone. Remember, Angie, women couldn't even have a credit card without a male co-signer."

I began to remember my mom's frustration driving from bank to bank trying to get a loan. She couldn't without a man's signature, yet she started and was running a hundred-thousand-dollar business, by herself. "Maybe it's time I go back to counseling," I said with a smile.

"Well, I'll join you. I still have issues with my parents, too. Who doesn't?"

"I do admire her, but I'd kinda like to come home to someone at night. You know, when I get an award for writing I'd like to share it with someone."

"What am I, chopped liver?" she laughed. "I know what you mean."

"Julie, you're always my date. It would be nice after a date to be able to sleep with my date," I teased.

"And when you say sleep, I know you mean sleep. You little virgin!" she teased back. "Heaven forbid you actually have sex with a man."

I smiled with pride. "I'm saving myself for someone special. And besides that, it's saved me a lot of heartache."

"You're crazy. You should be out there having fun. You're single. You're free spirited."

"I did that in my early twenties. I'm almost thirty."

"And it's almost *nine*-thirty." She said checking her watch. "Should we get going?"

"We better." I stood and stretched. "Thanks for meeting me, slut."

Julie stood and faced me with a confused look and half grin. "Did you just call me a …"

Before she could finish, I started nodding my head and laughing.

"OK, Prudence. Oh, and say hi to your slut mother for me."

"Oh." I stood there with my mouth wide open.

"I'm kidding, but do say hi to your mom for me. I'll see you soon."

We hugged. "Drive carefully."

Chapter 28

JULIE AND I spent our last day in Loveland together. I struggled with my car. I kept grinding my gears and Julie kept making fun of me. We drove by the last place Stan and I lived, places I had worked, and where I had gone to school. While we were in front of my old high school, I couldn't get my car into gear.

Julie and I looked at each other and started laughing nervously.

I had it towed to a nearby shop, and we waited for the news.

"If it's going to take over two days to fix it, I'm going to sell it cheap and we'll take the bus back. Is that OK with you?" I asked Julie.

"Sure."

"I was going to sell it when I got back to Minnesota anyway. I'll be working three blocks from my new apartment. My plan is to walk to work for the exercise and to get more familiar with the downtown area. I want to learn the bus route. I'll save money, no car insurance, no gasoline, and no maintenance," I blabbed until I was out of breath. "Once I'm more secure at my new job, I'll get another car."

"Sounds great," she said and chuckled. "We seem to move right along at the same pace. I already wrote up an ad to put in the paper to sell my car."

"You're kidding? Are you getting something right away?"

"I'm keeping my eyes open."

The mechanic stepped from behind the garage wall. "Angie, you wanna step over here with me so I can show you the estimate." He gave me an upside down wave to follow him.

I stood to follow him then turned smiling and gave Julie the upside down wave to follow *me*.

It was the clutch. It would take a few days to fix and would cost me around three hundred dollars. I decided to sell it to the mechanic. He said his stepson needed a good college car, and he trusted Honda and me. He gave me a fair price.

It was hard to say goodbye to my car. It used to be my home. That car kept me safe. If I could have wrapped my arms around it with out looking crazy, I would have.

"Angie, it's a car," Julie said.

"My car was better to me than most people. It never let me down."

"Until now."

"My car always knows what's best for me," I said in a little girl voice. "Now I don't have to put an ad in the paper, make arrangements for people to stop over to see it. It's done, sold, no waiting."

"Well, you're right about that," she said. "You bond more with your car than with people... men," she winked.

"It's safer," I smirked.

"You're sick."

We walked away from my car.

Chapter 29

OUR MONTH'S VACATION had turned into only two-and-a-half weeks. Once we made the decision, we were both eager to get back to our lives in Minnesota. We were almost home, about four hours away, when reality woke me up.

It was around three in the morning, and the half-empty bus had everyone sprawled across two seats sleeping. Something was waking me, slowly. I was dreaming about a lover and we were lying next to each other, with his hand rubbing up and down my inner thigh. I didn't want to wake up, it felt good. He was so warm. Before I could thoroughly enjoy the moment, I came fully awake and realized a stranger sitting across the isle had his foot between my legs, rubbing me. This brought me to complete consciousness, and I yelled, "Stop it!"

He quickly moved his foot from my body to the armrest on his seat, which I felt was still too close to me. I lay there waiting for him to touch me again. I wanted him to try it while I was awake and ready for it. So I waited with my eyes shut, slightly opening them on occasion. I was unable to see this man in the dark, except he seemed middle aged and wore a hat low on his head. My heart was pounding, and my adrenaline was forcing me to fantasize about what I would do to him if he dared touch me again. I wanted to beat the fuck out of him, with no remorse and no concern over what might happen to me.

After about five minutes, I couldn't take it anymore. Something had to be done about this, and it didn't look like he was going to make his move again. Disappointed in a way because I didn't get the chance to crush his balls with my knee, I got up and told the bus driver he had to kick a man off the bus.

"Why?" he asked.

"Because I was sleeping, and he had his foot between my legs rubbing me!"

"Who is he?" he asked checking his rearview mirror to see who I was referring to, like he thought it was my boyfriend I was mad at or fighting with and wanted to kick off the bus.

"I don't know who he is!"

"OK, I'll take care of it."

I went back to my same seat, only two seats behind the bus driver, and waited. I looked to his mirror. In the light from an on coming car, I could see his pitted dark skin and the look of sadness on his face. I was really surprised by everything that was happening. I was being strong. And I was proud.

The bus driver took the next exit, an exit not on the route. He drove about two miles and stopped at a twenty-four hour convenience store. He parked on the street and ran inside. While I was sitting there Julie woke up and asked, "What's going on?"

Still angry, I said, "I'll talk to you about it later."

The bus driver walked back in and pointed to me. "Will you come with me please," he said.

I got up and left the bus with him. On our short walk from the bus to the store, he informed me he had called the police and they were on their way.

This man did more for me than he will ever know. Although a part of me was being strong, there was part of me that felt I was making a mountain out of a molehill. Big deal his foot was between your legs. It's not like he was raping you, or fingering you in your sleep. It was just his foot.

But this bus driver helped me be strong. I only wanted the pervert dropped off at the next bus stop. It was he who stopped the bus, it was he who called the police, and it was he who helped me as a woman fight for the respect I deserved. He didn't talk much, and when the police came he stepped back and let them do their job.

I was in the store with a male police officer, and he told me they were going to wait for a female officer to talk to me. While we waited, Julie tried to come into the store, but the police wouldn't let her. I saw the look of hurt on her face. She knew something bad happened to me, and she wanted to be there for me. I watched a police officer walk her back to the bus.

When the female officer got there, she did the questioning. She was petite and seemed pretty under all her makeup. I pressed charges. The bus driver went with the police to escort the man off the bus. He was put into a police car and driven away. When the whole thing was over, an hour-and-a-half had passed.

I sat in the front seat with Julie. She watched me cry and listened as I tried to sort it all out. "See, Julie. Why does it keep happening? I don't ask for it. I'm not looking for it."

"I don't know, Ang," she said seriously. She rubbed my shoulder and gave me a hug. "Angie, maybe you were the only one strong enough on this bus to take it, so God picked you." She continued, whispering. "Maybe if we were on time we would have been in a terrible accident and we all would have been killed. Maybe the bus driver was getting sleepy. Maybe we would have been in a head on with a semi. I don't know." She started to cry. "I don't know why."

It took me a minute to understand what she was saying, and in some ways, it was too soon to think like that. But I had strong faith, and maybe there was something greater happening than I realized. It reminded me of the snow God made to cover my car and protect me from perpetrators.

"Maybe it's just that you were the one who would stop the bus."

I squeezed her hand to thank her. I didn't want to talk anymore. I snuggled in next to Julie and let her hold me while I cried. I knew later I'd turn it into something positive, but for now, it still hurt. I was still shaken. And I wanted to be with my pain for a while.

The bus driver helped me that morning and I thanked him. I didn't know a man could be so strong. Every stop we made he had to deal with people being upset because we were late. It didn't seem to bother him. It bothered me more. I felt like it was all my fault. Julie was quick to set me straight. "It is all that man's fault who did that to you. It's not your fault!" she said.

The anger, hurt, and passion from what happened to me on the bus went straight into my first piece for the newspaper. There was an overwhelming response. My job was secure.

Chapter 30

TIME WAS FLYING. Almost a year had passed since I started at the paper and I still loved it. It was where I wanted to be for the rest of my life or until I had nothing left to write about. Mary, my boss, liked my work and me. I always wrote about women's issues. My writing was for women, though I secretly hoped men would read it too. Some did.

I had my own office and everything that comes with it. It was small, in the back of the building, with a brick wall and an alley for a view. The building stood twelve stories high and my office was on the ninth floor. It didn't take long for me to find the rooftop, where I spent most of my breaks. I was so high up, ideas flew to me.

I walked onto the rooftop and realized what a beautiful day it had become, a gray day, which was my favorite, kind of misty and hazy. I loved it on the rooftop, maybe because I was usually alone. I discovered I loved to be alone, with people all around me, yet nobody noticing me or talking to me. I felt happy and free on the rooftop separated from the world of problems.

I looked down into the streets watching all the beautiful, colorful people, hurrying to wherever they were off to. I heard a drumbeat from the other side of the roof echoing throughout the city streets. I walked to the other side and saw a couple of younger people playing drums and having a great time. A few people gathered around them and started to dance. I smiled wishing I had a camera to capture the moment, then realized the memory was already captured.

From the rooftop, I could see a strip club. They called it a gentlemen's club which made no sense. True gentlemen would not go to a place where they are encouraged to abuse and harass women.

I sat and watched the physically, but not emotionally, beautiful women walking to their dehumanizing job. I could pick them out. They carried themselves like they were famous movie stars, but really they were young women paid to be naked and humiliated. The sad thing was they had to pretend to enjoy it. I know I had.

The men went in with their pockets full of money, hoping to buy some kind of treatment to make them feel worthy of sexual attention. The women seemed ugly to me because they had given up on women and fallen to the side of the morally corrupt men. If a woman was there putting herself in that place of degradation, she deserved to be degraded. On the other hand, I knew there had to be a reason. There had been for me.

The memory of Joan came to me and gave me a chill. I grabbed my shoulders and rubbed my arms. I thought about the differences in every woman's life. How Joan's life seemed opposite from the women's entering the club, but these women were also living their lives for men: only in a different way.

Chapter 31

I REMEMBERED MEETING Joan.

Mary called me into her office with a grin of satisfaction. "You're going to Thorton to do a story."

I was already working on a family law case and going to court every day. I said nothing and waited for her to continue.

"A woman named Joan Climb called us with a story, but she said you're the only one she'll talk to," she said with that same proud smile. "How does that make you feel?"

"What's the story? Why me?" I asked.

"Oh, Angie, we've been trying to get one of these women to talk for a long time. She was married to a well known doctor at Central Medical. He left her for a young woman, or should I say girl. It's a process; they all go through it up there. So I want you to talk to other women too, not just Climb. Try to talk to some of her friends, anyone you can. Here's her address and number," Mary said handing me an index card. "You'll be staying at the Holiday Inn downtown. Here is your reservation number and the keys to your rental car. It's downstairs ready to go. You have a week."

"What about the story I'm on?" I asked.

"It's been dropped."

"Why?"

"We want this."

"Can't you send Jill or Adrienne to Thorton?"

"She wants you. She said she's a big fan and believes only you can do her justice."

"And it can't wait a week?"

"No."

"Somebody has to finish the story I'm on. It's significant."

After a brief staring contest she said, "Give me what you've got. I'll finish it."

Now I was the one grinning, "OK…I'll go get it."

"By the way, Joan's expecting you this afternoon," she said trying to rush me as I walked out the door.

On the hour-and-a-half drive, I thought about what an important assignment this was for the paper and all women. I was intimidated because she asked for me, and I wanted to do the best I'd ever done because of it.

I pulled into the driveway, grabbed my bag, and walked to the front door where she stood to greet me. She was a slender, attractive woman with auburn hair. She looked like she was in her early fifties.

"You made it."

"Yes. I hope I didn't keep you waiting."

"Oh, no," she said. "You're younger than I pictured."

"I've crammed a lot into these years."

"I know you have. I'm Joan."

"Angie." My bag traded hands and I shook hers.

We walked into the house. "Well, Angie, let's sit in the living room. It's more comfortable." She walked away and I followed. She turned around and handed me a piece of paper. "These are the questions I want you to ask me."

I smiled behind her back and read some of the questions. We sat down in her peach-colored room and she poured me some tea from the tray sitting on the table. "Here you are. Let's begin." She handed me my cup.

The questions weren't far off from what I was planning, so I went along with her. I set my tape recorder next to the tea and pushed the record button. The first question read, "What were you going to school for?"

"First, can we talk a little about your life right now and what made you want to talk about this?" I asked.

"The questions will lead us every place we need to go. So let's just start with number one."

I gave her a questioning look.

"I'm sorry. I guess I'm a little nervous," she admitted.

"It's OK. I'll do your questions." I could tell this was very important to her, so I wanted to be careful. "Did you and your husband meet in college?" I asked.

She relaxed. "Yes, we did."

"What did you study in college?"

Joan's eyes lit up. "I've always loved children," she said. "I was going to be a school teacher. Bill was going to be a doctor." She paused. "I remember he used to pick me up for dates in this beat-up old Pinto." She looked out the window. Children were playing across the street. Their laughter and screams seemed distant.

"He used to promise me the world. He'd say, 'One day, I'll be a great doctor and you'll have everything you want. We'll have a nice house, expensive cars, and take exotic vacations.' But that's not why I loved him." She turned back my way and leaned against the window. "I didn't care if he pumped gas for a living, but then I guess he wouldn't have been Bill. He always had a fire inside him. To think small was never good enough for him. He wanted the best of everything. And I gave him the best of what I had."

"When did you marry?"

"I became pregnant, so we planned for the wedding. It was about a year after we met. I lost the baby about a week before the ceremony. I had already dropped out of college, and Bill said he still wanted to marry me." She gave me a grim smile and sighed. "He felt since I had lost the baby, I could get another job, fulltime, and he could cram in more school while I supported us. So that's what I did."

"How was that, working two jobs?"

"It was hard." She sat down in the chair across from me and took a sip of her tea. "I did laundry for a nursing home full time, and I worked as a cashier and waited tables at night. But the one good thing about it was I could get out of the house and away from Bill. All that studying made him crabby." She giggled. Then serious she said, "Don't ever let a man have you."

"When did things get better, easier?"

"Don't you mean when did the money start coming in?" she said and smiled.

"Yes," I said and smiled back. I kept repeating those words in my mind. Don't ever let a man have you. Don't ever let a man have you.

"It wasn't easier, just different. I didn't have to work anymore, but I wanted to. He assured me he needed me at home. So I stayed home. I took a cooking class, but it was more for him than me. He thought I should improve my skills at home. He wanted me to be better for him. I lost another baby around that time."

Her grandfather clock chimed. We both turned our attention to it until it stopped.

"I left him, shortly after, for about a month. I got a job, moved into an apartment and things were going well. I was happy, except for people who told me I was a bad wife and a bad woman for leaving my husband." She slowly shook her head. "But then Central Hospital in Thorton wanted him. This was a huge, huge step for him. He was on his way and didn't want to go alone. He promised me things would be easier for me. He promised we could start a family right away. I wanted many children, and he knew that. He said I could go to school if I wanted to and become a teacher. And he promised we would get along better."

I knew the direction this was headed. I took a drink of tea trying to stay detached. I wondered how to read tea leaves. I wondered the true name of her peach-colored walls: Conch Peach… Peach sunset… Alpenglow…

"So I went with him. I still loved him, and that old fire had returned to our relationship. When we got to Thorton, I believed I had done the right thing. He bought me a car to go to school. We lived in a beautiful four-bedroom home, and we were anxious to fill it with children. After Timothy was born everything stopped. He wanted me at home again, which was OK, since I wanted to be there for Tim. After two failed pregnancies, I cherished my baby. He was everything to me.

"So everything came second to Tim, including Bill. I had always been second to his career, so I didn't feel I was being unfair. I was still there for Bill. It's just that Tim came first. Bill became jealous of Tim. It was strange. He never wanted to be around me. Now that I was happy and had Tim, Bill was unhappy. He said we couldn't have any more kids. I argued, then lied, saying I didn't want anymore either. I knew I'd keep trying. What would he do, make me have an abortion?" She looked as if asking me. "Close. About a week after a heated argument he told me he made an appointment for me for a routine check up. I was fine but agreed a check up wouldn't hurt me. The day of my 'checkup,'" she made quotations with her fingers. "I was rushed into emergency surgery and had a hysterectomy. I was twenty-eight years old. Figure that one out," she said to me. "Bill was happy. I spent months in depression. Tim was the only light in my day."

I was shocked. "Joan, did you hire an attorney? Did anyone investigate?"

She looked straight into my eyes. "Nobody would touch it... Nobody! In fact, they assured me Central would never make a mistake like that, and if the surgery was done, it was needed. I started seeing a therapist who also assured me. I thought I was going crazy. It became easier to believe, so I did, for my own sanity." Again she said, "Don't ever let a man have you."

"I don't know how it happened, but I was brainwashed, maybe because he was paying for my therapy. I didn't see it until now. By the time Tim was headed to college, I had seen marriage after marriage fall apart. It usually happened when the doctor hit complete security at Central and a younger woman was always involved, often a fresh young nurse. I was taught to believe the ex-wives had gone crazy, a couple even ended up in hospitals. They didn't go crazy. They were being pumped with medications and released only after the divorce was well on its way. The doctors just wanted them out of the way so they could do what they wanted, and get away with it. The women, just like me, gave themselves to their husbands and families. We did what we thought we were supposed to do, what we were taught to do. We gave these men our whole lives."

After a moment of silence she continued, "I'll never forget the day it happened. God, I was lost. Tim was in college, and I was looking forward to the time I'd have with Bill. I imagined weekend getaways, longer vacations, and quiet romantic dinners. I was going to take the money I'd saved from the allowance Bill had given me to join a health club. I wanted to lose some of the weight Bill liked to mention. I had been checking into some things that I'd always wanted to do, but had put on hold for my family. I thought now was the perfect time.

"I came home from the store, and there was a green sports car in the driveway. I honked to the young woman sitting in the driver's seat to move. She sat there as if she didn't understand. So I parked in the street, grabbed my groceries and went inside. I honestly thought Tim had come home for a surprise visit and that was his new girlfriend in the car. I rushed into the house and saw Bill coming down the stairs with his hands full of clothes. His luggage was already sitting at the door. I assumed he was in a hurry and going out of town on business. I put the groceries down to help him and dizziness came over me. I knew even before he said it. He was leaving me. I remember sitting down on the stairs, in his way, and crying. It's all I could do. At that moment everything made sense. I understood the woman in the car was his girlfriend, and I understood the ex-wives hadn't gone crazy. I knew I too would be one of those wives. But I decided not to fight like the others; I didn't want to end up in a mental hospital. I didn't want to get a reputation of being one of those ex-wives.

"So I'm doing OK. I work. I live here." She looked around. "Not the greatest place, but it's enough for me. And now everyday I wake up I hurt." Joan started crying. "I really believed Bill and I were partners for life. My life is almost over, and I have nothing to show for it but a grownup son, and an ex-husband. I never became a teacher. I never had the chance to have more kids. I never lived my life, I lived Bill's. All the things he said he wanted to give me he's now giving her. They take exotic vacations. They have a huge beautiful home, better than the one we lived in for all those years, but the thing that hurts the most is the fact that she's pregnant and they are planning to have a large family. Who knows, maybe it will happen to her too. I wouldn't want it to, though. As angry and hurt as I am, I wouldn't want it to happen to any woman. Maybe that's why I'm talking to you."

Joan and I talked every day while I was working on the article. We drove around to the schools Tim attended, the arenas where he played hockey, the home they lived in all those years, and the homes of her friends who went through the same thing before her. She told me more about their stories and more of her own experiences as a Central wife.

My article was almost complete. I had to get back to the office to finish. I said my good-byes to Joan and encouraged her to write a book. I felt the wives of all corporations could relate to her story and it might help them to know they are not alone. Joan said she'd consider it. She read the rough draft of my article and thanked me for doing it. "Angie, this means more to me than you'll ever know. Remember, don't ever let a man have you," she said with a stern look.

I smiled, gave her a hug, and headed back to the city.

A few months later, I was up for an award for that article. One of the greatest nights of my life was also one of my worst. While I was worrying about what to wear, Joan was picking out her best wine. While I was driving to the ceremony, Joan was drawing her bath. While I was talking with the other guests, Joan was lighting a candle. While I was seated and waiting with anticipation, Joan was soaking in her warm bath. And when I was accepting my award, Joan was accepting a bottle of pills followed by a toast with her favorite wine. When my night was over, Joan's life had ended. I reached over and turned the light off. Joan's candle had burned out.

Chapter 32

EVERY DAY FOR weeks, I watched the women walking into the strip club and decided I wanted to do a story about them. I came up with the ideas and had them approved. I'd never had an idea denied. Mary questioned some, but always gave me the go ahead. Those usually turned out to be the best stories. Mary liked my angle, so when I had this idea she OK'd it, though she was uncertain I could get the interviews and the information I needed to write the story.

I started my interviewing on a Wednesday afternoon. I approached the door of the club and wondered if anybody watching would mistake me for a dancer. I opened the door and went inside. The stage where the dancing took place was not visible from the entrance.

I stood looking around and an attractive woman asked, "Can I help you?"

"Yes, I called and talked to a man by the name of Steve. Is he here?"

"Oh, you're that woman who wants to interview the dancers."

"Well, yes, and other women who work here as well."

"Steve left. But he asked me to help you with anything you need."

I was surprised Steve would be so open with my interviewing the women. Though I was misleading in the type of article I would be writing. Steve obviously didn't research *me*.

"My name is Karen. I'm a bartender here."

"Thanks, Karen, I'm Angie. Can I start with you?"

"Sure, if you don't mind sitting at the bar. I have to work right now. I just ran down here to get some more pens. They always seem to disappear."

I followed her up a few stairs and to the right. The bar was empty with the exception of a couple men sitting off to one side. I walked to the other side of the bar to be alone. I set my bag on the stool next to me and reached in for my notebook, pen, and tape recorder. The music was loud, and I wasn't sure how well the recorder would pick up my conversation with Karen. I scribbled a few notes. My eyes were going to take a beating on this assignment. The place was dark. I didn't expect it to be like this in the afternoon.

Karen walked over and asked, "Can I get you something to drink?"

"A glass of water would be great. Thanks."

She set the water down in front of me, on a napkin. "I'll be right with you," she said.

"Take your time," I said. I turned to the stage and understood why my side of the bar was empty. I had to turn completely around to face the dance floor. I watched for a while. I didn't watch the dancing as much as I watched the men in the bar and the way they reacted. It made me ill to see what these women were doing. Part of me felt I could not do this story. I didn't know why this was so hard on me, but it was.

Maybe I'm not a good reporter. I take everything personally. I get too emotional about women's issues.

"OK. I got them all taken care of. I'm all yours, at least for a while," Karen said.

I decided to stop feeling sorry for these women and myself and just proceed with it. "Great!" I said. "I am going to be direct with my questions. If they offend you, I'm sorry, and you don't have to reply to every question if you don't feel comfortable. Shall we begin?"

"I'm ready!"

"Why are you working at a place like this?"

She looked a bit surprised, smiled and answered, "Well, I guess you mean with women dancing around naked. Well, the money is a lot better here. I've worked at other bars, and the men that come in here aren't much different, they just have more money. I've become used to the dancing. I'm good friends with most of the women who work here."

"Do you like it?"

"At first I really did. It was fun getting so much attention from men and being asked out often. But it got old. Now I hate that part of the job. I get harassed all the time by customers, even by some of the male employees." She put her hand up as if to stop me. "Please don't put that in the paper."

I shook my head.

"Now the only reason I enjoy it is because we women who work here make it fun for each other. We laugh at the men who come here. It really is disgusting to watch these men. But most of us are pretty close. We hang out, go shopping, go to the movies." She smiled then just as quickly she frowned. "It's like a different world working here, we see all sorts of things. I wish I could tell you some of the things that go on here, but you'd print it and I'd lose my job."

"Listen, I just want things better for women. I'm not here to exploit you and get you into trouble. When I'm finished with this article, every woman I interview will have the opportunity to read and change anything she doesn't like or feels would be a problem if it were to be printed. So don't worry, women mean more to me than a great story, even though I think this will be a great story," I said.

"Really, I'll be able to read it before it goes out?"

"Yes, absolutely."

She looked over her shoulder. "Op, I'm needed, I'll be right back."

She walked away and I watched her. She was thin which made her look taller though she was, only about 5'3". Her hair was red and her skin pale. Her eyes were bright green or blue, I couldn't tell in the lighting. Karen smiled a lot. She was very friendly and talked to people as if she'd known them for ages.

She walked back and asked, "Where were we?"

"If you could do anything for a living what would it be?" I asked.

"I've always wanted to have my own gym and teach gymnastics to children. I used to compete in high school, but never went any farther than that. Every fall I help a woman teach gymnastics. I'm the assistant coach. She has her own gym, and I guess I'm envious of her and what she has. I love children."

"Do you have any?"

"No," she said.

"How about a boyfriend?"

"No, I don't have one of those either. I had a boyfriend. I was in love, wanted to spend my whole life with him. He cheated on me more than once. I haven't been able to get serious about a man since."

"I'm sorry. How long ago was that?"

"Oh, I'd say about a year now. Don't get me wrong now, I do date. I'm just too afraid of commitment. It's hard to trust after that," she said.

"How long have you worked here?" I asked.

"Uh, I guess about the same, almost a year."

"Do you think they have anything to do with each other?"

"I don't know," she said, with the memories of the past starting to show on her face, "Maybe." She looked around the club and turned to me and said, "It's starting to fill up. I'm going to be rather busy the rest of the night. I work tomorrow too, if you want to come in."

"Well, actually, I will see you tomorrow, but I'll probably be talking to some of the other women. I'll be in and out for the next few days, maybe a week."

I reached for my bag to put my stuff back inside and turned to watch the dancers and the men fill the place up.

I noticed three other women I wanted to talk to. Two were dancers and one was a woman standing near the entrance selling beer from a big aluminum tub. I asked Karen about the woman selling beer. She said her name was Sara, and she hardly talked to anybody. I got up and walked over to her. Her face was full of anger and sadness. She intimidated me in a way.

"Hi. My name is Angie. I'm interviewing some of the women who work here. I'd be interested in talking with you some time this week. Do you work tomorrow?"

"Yes."

"Would it be OK to ask you some questions then?" I asked.

"That's fine, but I'll be working," she said, looking past me.

"OK, I'll see you tomorrow," I said. She didn't reply and I walked out the door. I was going to enjoy doing the interviewing. The women weren't different than most I'd known, just working in a different world than most women do.

Chapter 33

THE NEXT AFTERNOON I went in a little earlier so I could watch more of what goes on in the preparation of a Thursday night. Karen was already in, so I visited with her for a while at the bar. She set a mineral water down in front of me and asked, "So who are you talking to tonight?"

"Sara," I said.

"Really? I'm surprised. Like I said before, she doesn't talk to anybody. Oh, you know, I was thinking last night, you should talk to some of the guys who come in here, too."

A little surprised she seemed so interested, I said, "This article is going to be all about women: our thoughts and our feelings. But that's a good idea. I'll think about it. Thanks for the suggestion."

"Yeah, that way women can read about what idiots men can be, in case they don't already know," she added.

I smiled, raised my glass to my mouth, and turned to watch the dancers. I'd like to say the environment gave women an attitude about men, but I knew that was not the case. Women were mistreated wherever they went, no matter what job they had; in a place like this, though, to be treated like an object was expected.

Sara sneaked in without my noticing. I looked around the room and saw she was in a conversation with a man. She looked different. She was smiling and flirting with him. It was different from the impression she gave me yesterday evening. Maybe she was in a good mood. I saw him handing her his business card, and I was shocked by her reaction. She bent over holding her blond hair back with one hand and motioned him to put his card in her cleavage. He did and so she gave him a kiss. Her smile dissolved on her walk to her tub of beer. For the first time I noticed how large her breasts were, and I felt sorry for her.

Not knowing what to say, I stood up and walked over to her.

"Hi, Sara," I said, "How are you today?"

"Fine."

"Some of the girls here found it hard to believe you would talk to me. Are you still willing to do the interview?" I asked.

"I said I would, didn't I?"

"OK. Well, do you enjoy working here?" I asked.

"Yes, I love it."

"Why?"

"Well, I make great money, maybe even better than some of the dancers, and all I have to do is stand here. The men love me. I'm asked out all the time. I can pick and choose who and when. It's the best job I've ever had."

"I really don't understand what you mean by pick and choose. Do you date a lot of men who come in here?"

"Yes, I think most of us do."

"Do you ever date men who you meet outside of work?"

"No, not really. I have met some guys at parties, but it's all kind of related to this place," she said.

"So, you don't have a boyfriend?"

"No!" she said quickly as if to cut me off. Then just as suddenly she seemed to reconsider. "I do spend some time with one of the bosses."

"Do you have friends who work here?" I asked.

"No."

"All the women who work here, and you're not friends with any of them?"

"No, I don't like them. They're jealous of my body and the fact that I don't have to work as hard as they do. I just stand here and get more attention than them when they're dancing around sticking their asses and tits in men's faces and still don't make as much money as I do."

"So, it's all about money for you then?"

She laughed sarcastically, "What else is there?"

"What about love and respect, family and friends?"

"No such things," she looked down at the tub of beer.

"When you were a little girl, what did you fantasize about being when you got older?"

Before she could answer a young man with wavy brown hair walked up to us and asked her for a beer.

"That will be five twenty-five," she said.

He handed her six dollars "Keep the change," he said. "Can I touch them?" he added, staring at her breasts.

"Baby, you'd have to give me a lot more than a seventy-five cent tip to touch these," she said as she pushed her chest out toward him. The man walked away with a big grin on his face as though he'd gotten caught trying to get away with something.

"Do you ever wonder how men can respect women after hearing something like that come out of a woman's mouth!" I said to her before I had a chance to bite my tongue. This woman disgusted me. I didn't even want to call her a woman. Before she had a chance to respond I thanked her for the talk and walked away.

I left the club and walked down the street feeling insecure about doing this assignment. I took it all so personally. What one woman does affects all women.

Chapter 34

WHEN I GOT home my phone was ringing. I picked it up, "Hello?"

"I was about to hang up. I figured you weren't home yet. So how'd it go today?" Julie asked.

I took a deep breath and exhaled, "Oh, I don't know."

"Come on, what's wrong?"

"Well, I interviewed this one woman, Sara, today and she really upset me. You wouldn't believe what goes on. And you know me, I take everything so personally. It hurts my feelings to see women like this. I need a different angle."

"You need a different angle? Let's go back there. I'll go with you, and we'll just watch what goes on. Don't bring your tape recorder or your notebook. We'll just go hang out for a while tonight when it's busy. You wanna?"

"You know, that's a good idea. Let's get a bite to eat before we go. Let me think, what's over there... "

"How about that one place on Marquette? Oh, what's the name of it, you know, it's kind of new?"

"Oh, I know where you're talking about. Yeah, let's go there. Give me about an hour. Do you want to come over here first and go together or do you want to meet on the six-fifteen bus?" I asked.

"I'll come get ya, I got a car."

"You bought a car?"

"Well, I'm thinking about it. I'm test-driving this one. I know the guy. He said I could keep it over night."

"Did you find yourself a boyfriend?" I teased.

We both laughed, and I knew a night out with her was really all I needed. We hung up, and I headed to the shower.

Chapter 35

WE WERE SITTING near the entrance by a pay phone. Julie noticed her first and pointed her out to me. There was a woman with long straight brown hair using the phone and crying. I knew the tears couldn't be mistaken for anything other than hurt from a man. After a short time she hung up and started walking toward us. She wiped away her tears with her hand. As she passed she looked right at me, and my heart went out to her. I looked at Julie. She was writing quickly on a napkin. I couldn't help laughing at how much alike we were. She looked up at me when she finished with her thought and smiled back. "I know what you're thinking," she said.

"OK, what?"

"You think I look like you, writing my thoughts down. But that woman gave me a great idea for a song."

"Really! She gave me an idea for a story too, in case I can't pull this one off," I said.

"Well, all I know is I'm glad I don't have to compete with you in the same career. I feel sorry for anyone who does. You're a great writer, and if anyone can make the strip club story work, it's you," she said.

I smiled to thank her. "I hate having doubts, but I do."

"Who doesn't?"

When we got to the club, Julie and I headed to the back and sat at the bar. Julie started flirting with the bartender right away. He was in good spirits and probably enjoyed the female customers for a change. He was slender and handsome, wearing the required tuxedo. He seemed to be wearing more hairspray than Julie and I put together. We both ordered mineral water, and he gave us a hard time about not drinking. It didn't take long for the DJ to find his way over to the bar. He was about twenty-seven years old, average looking, but his eyes were so bright they seemed to glow. He wanted to see what all the commotion was about, two women sitting at the bar of a men's club. I didn't think that was the only thing that brought him over to us. He recognized Julie from when she first started out touring at local clubs, so they talked for a while.

"So you're the one doing the interviewing, aren't you?" the bartender asked me.

"That's right."

"Well, the girls have been talking a lot about it, always wondering if they'll be picked for an interview. You know how these women are; they want to be stars. That's why they work here. They think they're going to be discovered."

"How do you know why they work here?" I asked.

"Because I'm dating one of the dancers, and that's how she thinks."

"Well, what do you think?"

"What, are you interviewing me now?" he asked grinning at me. I glared back, so he replied. "No, I don't think anybody will be discovered here. Maybe someone will discover what sluts they all are."

"If you really felt that way you wouldn't be dating one of the dancers."

"I didn't say I was going to marry her. I just spend time with her. There's a big difference."

"So in other words, you're just fucking her."

"Well, I guess you could say that," he answered, and I walked away.

Julie and the DJ had moved to a table. He must have been on a break because he had been next to her practically since we sat down at the bar. I did have to question his motives. Julie is already in the music business, and he is a DJ at a strip club. I do know Julie would never let someone use her, or walk on her so I wasn't concerned. I walked over to their table and sat down. He said he had to get back to work, so he stood and asked if he could come back and talk more later.

"I'm sorry, don't let me scare you off," I said feeling as if I interrupted something.

"No, I really have to get back. Besides, I want to talk to you later, too," he said, and rushed off.

"Everybody knows about me doing the interviewing here," I said.

"I just think everybody wants to be interviewed by you, even the DJ," Julie said.

"How did that go, you and the music man. Do you like him?" I asked.

"Yeah, it's strange, I do, but I can't respect him working in a place like this. Oh, and get this, he goes by DJ. That's his name."

"You're kidding!"

"Nope," she said. We both laughed.

"Jul, have you been watching what goes on here?"

"Yeah, and the bouncers are just as bad as the customers, they just hide behind their jobs. I can't believe these women do this for a living. It's really sad. Let's talk to some of them."

"What do you mean?" I asked.

A dancer walked by and Julie asked her to come over and talk to us.

"I'm not paid to talk!" she said very rudely to Julie.

Julie replied, "Yeah, but wouldn't you like to be!"

I sat there with my mouth wide open, shocked, but pleased by Julie's witty response. "Julie! You can't fight with these women. I have to get the interviews!"

"I'm sorry," she said. "I couldn't resist. She was rude."

"I know, but… "

A woman walked over and asked if she could join us. Julie removed her jacket from the chair as the woman pulled it out and sat down. She was pretty with dark, shoulder-length hair, bright blue eyes, and tan skin. She was wearing a sleeveless blouse that showed her muscular arms. It was obvious she lifted weights. "Hi, my name's Jody. I'm a bartender here," she said.

We introduced ourselves and talked most of the night away. She had just gotten off her shift. She heard I was doing interviews for a newspaper article and wanted to find out more about who I was and why I was interviewing. She was so down to earth anyone would like her. She opened up and told us all about the man she lived with for two years. He was a gambling addict. He lied to her, and took everything from her, including her heart.

She said she had been financially secure when the relationship started. As the money faded, so did his love. Now she was working as a bartender for what she considered a bunch of male chauvinist pigs. She said she didn't mind too much because it always kept her reminded, it was always fresh in her head, just what assholes men could be. So she talked to them, watched them and kept in mind why she chose to be alone, and working this slime job in the first place.

While we were talking, Jody would call dancers over to introduce us. Many of them took their breaks at our table. I got the feeling Jody was well liked by everyone and had probably been there the longest.

Julie and I left just before closing. We both enjoyed the night, and I thanked her for getting me out for the evening. I knew which of the dancers I wanted to interview: Rebecca, Bonnie, and Veronica. I talked with them a while, and they were all willing to do the interview with me. There was one woman named Kay who wanted nothing to do with me. She was the same one Julie had mouthed off to earlier, so I couldn't blame her. She had an attitude. She was tall with short dark hair and a slender body, acting like she was better than everyone. What stuck out the most about her, were the dark circles under her eyes. I really wanted to talk with her, but she didn't give me the chance.

Chapter 36

I WENT TO the club just before Rebecca got off work. While I waited, I sat at the dark wooden and brass bar and talked to Jody who was bartending that night. It was around seven o'clock, and she had just started her shift. She seemed rushed and irritated.

"What's going on, Jody?" I asked.

"The jerk that worked before me left this place a mess. He always does." She looked around. "Angie, I'm really getting tired of this place."

"So why don't you leave?"

"I've been seriously thinking about it." She ran her fingers through her hair, pulling it from her face. "I'm not happy here, but I feel stuck. The money's good, and most of my friends work here."

"Maybe you and your friends should put your money together and start your own business," I suggested.

She laughed. "Could you imagine all of us leaving at the same time on our busiest night? I'd do it just to see all their faces. Wouldn't that be a hoot?"

It was nice to see her mood change, though I knew she didn't take my idea seriously. A man across the bar called to her. She walked away still chuckling at the idea of a walkout.

Rebecca was on stage dancing to Michael Jackson's "Keep it in The Closet," so I turned to watch. Her dancing seemed less confident than I'd seen before. A middle-aged blonde man on the left side of the stage was holding up a twenty-dollar bill. I expected her to hurry to it, but instead she avoided him. When he began whistling for her attention, she left the stage before the song was over. Bonnie had been waiting back stage for her turn to go on, so she moved in to cover for Rebecca. When Bonnie moved toward the guy with the twenty-dollar bill, he put it back into his wallet, finished the last of his drink and walked over to the bar where I was sitting. He carried himself like he was superior to everyone around him. I didn't like him. Rebecca came out wearing a brown leather bomber jacket, and a pair of jeans; her hair was pulled up under a baseball cap. I barely recognized her when she grabbed me, hard, by the arm and tried to lead me to the door.

Upset, I stopped, pulled free, and said, "Rebecca! What do you think you're doing?"

She ignored me and continued walking. I followed her. When I got out the front door, there was silence under the street light. The smell of exhaust stuck in the cool, thick air. It was getting colder.

Rebecca was waiting for me. Before I could say anything she stepped in front of me. I could see terror in her pale face. Her voice trembled when she asked, "Can we go someplace? Please! I'll drive."

"Rebecca. Are you OK?" I asked.

"I need to get out of here." We started walking to her car in the parking ramp when a man who had just come out of the club started calling her by name. She ignored him and walked a little faster. I turned around to look. It was the same man who tried to give her the twenty.

"Who's the guy?" I asked.

She unlocked her door, then mine with her power switch. We both got in and she locked the doors with the same button. After a long exhale she answered, "Oh, just some guy I had a fling with." Rebecca started the car. "I'm sorry I freaked out. It's just that I haven't seen him since it happened." She put her car in reverse, backed out of the space, and we were on our way.

I was afraid because she seemed to be. I was concerned and wanted to know more. "So where are we going?" I asked.

"I'm sorry. You mind if we go to a bar? I could use a drink."

"No, that's fine, but find one quiet enough to talk."

"It'll be perfect. You'll love it," she assured me. Her delicate hands were clutching the steering wheel. The closer we got to our destination, the more she relaxed.

The place was quiet with soft lighting. Its decor seemed outdated, done in pinks, grays, and blacks. There was a dance floor, but I couldn't imagine anyone dancing on it. It looked to have been a classy club at one time.

I followed her straight-line march to the bar where she ordered a shot of whisky and a whiskey and coke. I ordered a mineral water and paid for all three. We took our drinks to a booth in a corner and started with the interview. I took out my notebook and pen. I wrote Rebecca on the top with the date.

Rebecca took her coat and hat off letting her hair fall from beneath it. "Can we talk about other things for a while? I'm kind of distracted," Rebecca said.

"Sure." I pushed my notebook to the side and asked, "Is it that man from the club?"

"I really don't want to talk about it," Rebecca said. She finished the last of her drink and snapped her fingers at the only server in the bar who was wiping off a nearby table.

The server, irritated, left the rag on the table and took her time walking over to us. "You need something?" Her voice was rough and raspy, like that of a fifty-year smoker, which she may have been.

"No!" Rebecca said, snotty, then started laughing. "Yes. I want a Coke and whiskey, I mean a whiskey and Coke," and started laughing again.

"Get it yourself!"

"No, no, I'm sorry. Please? Here!" Rebecca pleaded reaching into her purse. "I'll give you fifty dollars if you'll serve me all night," she said, pulling a fifty from her wallet.

"No." The server turned and walked away.

I was embarrassed and wanted to leave. "Rebecca, maybe we should do this another time," I said, starting to put away my notebook.

Rebecca reached across the table and held onto my forearm with both of her cold hands. "We don't have to do the interview tonight, but please don't leave me." She let go of my arm and stood up. "I'll go get my own drink. Please stay."

"OK," I said.

Rebecca walked up to the bar to get her drink. While she was waiting, she walked over to the server and tried to hand her the fifty. The server refused. I could tell Rebecca was trying to apologize. She walked back to the bar, got her drink and came back to sit down.

"Money doesn't mean anything to that woman!" Rebecca said.

"Rebecca, before you drink any more, do you have a safe way home?" I asked. "I don't have a car or I'd drive you home," I added.

"How about you take my car, drive me home and I'll call you in the morning to pick it up," she asked.

"You do plan on getting drunk."

"Only if you stay with me," Rebecca said looking into my eyes.

"So tell me about that guy," I said.

"Let's do the interview," she interrupted.

"I'd rather you were sober."

"I'm OK, let's do it."

I started asking her my usual questions. "Why do you work at the club?"

She looked serious and said, "Well..." and suddenly burst out laughing, hardly able to get a word out. "OK... OK... you're right... Let's talk about something... else," getting words out between her hysterical laughing. She looked up still laughing; her face was red and her blue eyes watering. "I know! Let's go dance!" She grabbed my hand and we headed to the dance floor.

The only other people in the club were two older, out-of-shape men sitting at the bar. She stepped right between them, resting a hand on each of their thighs. "Excuse me, bartender? Will you please put some good dancing music on? We wanna dance. How about something by, y'know, the artist that used to be Prince?" She laughed and led the way to the dance floor.

When we got on the dance floor she started dancing sleazy. I stood there for a minute then glanced at the bar. The two men were staring at her, smiling as if they were dogs panting. I reached over and stopped her with a hand on each of her shoulders. "Rebecca I didn't come here to dance or to ride on this roller coaster of yours. I came to get an interview with you. If you're not interested, I'll find someone who is." I walked off the dance floor. She followed. I started getting my things together when she turned me around to look at her.

"Can't you see I need help?" she said about to cry.

"Yes," I answered "but I don't see you wanting it."

"I do, I need to talk to someone, someone I can trust. I figure I can trust you. I don't want to talk about your stupid article. I want to talk about me." The tears in her eyes were about to overflow.

"OK," I said. "Let's sit down and talk." The server brought over a mineral water for me and a whisky and Coke for Rebecca. The guys from the bar bought them for us. Rebecca looked to me as if to ask for permission, I nodded my head and she began to drink it. She turned and held her glass up to the men as if to say cheers, then took another sip.

The drinking was beginning to mellow her, her movements and words were slowing. "Angie. Y'know that guy at the club?"

"Yes," I said.

"He's a cop."

"Really? Does he hang out there?" I asked.

"Yeah, I guess he does. But I haven't seen him for a while."

"Since the two of you had an affair?"

"Yeah, right." She took another sip from her drink and began crying. "Angie, he raped me!"

"What!"

"He's married, too," she added. She tried to laugh as if to stop the tears but couldn't.

"Did you go to the police?" I realized what a dumb question it was after I asked it.

"He is the police."

"When did it happen?"

"About a month ago," she said, using the backs of her hands to wipe her tears. "He took me home because my car was in the shop."

"What happened?" I asked.

"He was still on duty and in uniform. It happened in the front seat of his squad car."

"My God, Rebecca; I'm sorry."

"And there's nothing I can do about it. He's a cop and I'm a... I'm a... whore."

"Rebecca, you're not a whore!"

"You don't know my past. Everyone else does, and they all think I am. Because of that, you and I both know what it would come down to. He's a married cop who was seduced by a stripper. Then he tried to end it and the stripper cries rape. Don't I still deserve to choose if I want to or not?"

"Yes, you do deserve to decide. Why didn't you want to sleep with him if you sleep around like you say."

"Angie it wasn't like that! God!" She raised her voice. "Maybe in the right situation I would have wanted him, but not that night. My car broke down on the way to work so I was late. The money sucked that night, so I worked late trying to make it up. And some drunk guy pulled me off the stage, and I hurt my knee. That's one of the reasons the cops were there that night in the first place. Not that they didn't stop by often the way it was. But that night they were called. So you can understand I was in no mood. I just wanted to go home.

"But under different circumstances you may have wanted him?" I knew I was sounding callous, but I could tell she was feeling she deserved it in some way because of her past, and I wanted her to get to the truth of the matter.

"It wasn't sex, OK!" she said crying loudly. "It was something else!"

"What do you mean?"

"I mean it wasn't sex he took from me. It wasn't sex. It wasn't even fucking. It was something else. He took something away from me that night...He really hurt me."

"Did you go to the doctor?" I asked.

"For what? A hurt ego, a broken heart, a dead spirit, or the bruises on my arms and legs?"

I couldn't comment. I could only remember those same feelings after being raped by my husband.

"And what if I did go to the doctor or police, I'd just get raped again."

We sat in silence for a while as if trying to decide what to do. It truly seemed hopeless. I felt the only thing she could do was file a report and try to recover. I felt sorry for her. She knew the bed she made for herself. But we both knew a lot of her bed was made for her just because she was a woman.

"Is it a moral issue? Did I deserve it?"

"No. It is not a moral issue. You did not deserve it."

"He probably picked me out. The way I lived was no secret. Anyone could ask and they'd get a straight answer. It's not that I was proud. It's just, I had nothing to hide. I liked men. I liked sex. What's wrong with that? I'm single." She went on. "I didn't go to work for a couple nights after it happened. When I went back in to work Veronica asked me if I slept with the cop. I said, 'No!' It was the first time I lied about sex and for whose protection?"

"Rebecca, how did you start working at the club anyway?" I asked and reached into my bag to turn on my recorder. Then I pulled out a Kleenex and handed it to her so she wouldn't know. I wanted honesty. I didn't want her to feel I was interviewing her.

"Oh, that's another sad story." She smiled and she started to tear the Kleenex into little pieces. "I was living away from home with this man I was in love with. We had been together for about five years and talk of marriage was always there. I didn't want to do it because I was afraid. I really didn't know anybody who was happily married, and I guess in a way I just wasn't sure. My mother became sick, and she really needed me to be with her. So I left my boyfriend for a while to be with her, about five hours away. It was a family emergency. I was needed. I was gone for about two weeks.

"The whole time I was away I kept thinking about him and how he wanted to marry me. I loved him with all my heart, so while I was gone I made the decision I was going to marry and spend the rest of my life with him. I was going to put all my fears aside and trust him. On my way home I felt a sense of relief. I'd finally made the decision and couldn't wait to get home and tell him. I knew he'd be so excited because that's what he'd always wanted.

"When I got home I saw his face and could tell something was wrong. My walls had come down on the trip, and he had a hold of my heart. But at that moment my walls were building themselves back up. I asked, "What?"

He wouldn't answer. After the quiet staring had lasted a few minutes, he finally spoke. "I went to a strip bar while you were gone."

"Why?" I asked.

He continued as though I hadn't spoken. "And I slept with one of the strippers."

"The kind of hurt I felt at that moment lasts a lifetime. It took five years for me to let him into my heart, and I guess it was just too much time, he couldn't wait anymore." She looked down at the torn Kleenex and pushed it to the side. "I made him sleep on the couch until he found a place to live and that was the end of it. My mother treated me like shit because of it; she thought he was such a nice guy. She didn't feel like it was that big a deal. Well, it was a big deal to me. I don't want a man to do that to me. I'm going to be faithful to him, and I want the same in return. What's so hard about that? Why do they make it so damn hard," Rebecca said.

"I don't know," I agreed with her.

"So anyway, after he moved out I got this job and started being just the same way as the girl who ruined it for me, the same thing that broke us up. The message I got from my mom and the hurt from it all made me think love isn't important, time isn't important. I was with him five years. That woman was probably with him for five hours, and he gave her something that was precious to me. That's what guys wanted, and I wanted a guy. I want to be loved, so here I am." Rebecca smiled at me with her watering eyes. "I'm here doing the same thing that hurt me so badly. I sleep with men I know are married or have girlfriends, for no reason other than if you can't beat 'em, join 'em..."

"The only one you're hurting is yourself and other women. Why would you want to do that? We need to stick together. We need to look out for each other," I said.

"Why should a few women be that way, sticking together, when so many don't care?" Rebecca asked.

"Because it's right," I said. "Rebecca, before you had that relationship with the man who cheated on you, what did you want to do with your life? What were your dreams?" I asked.

"You know, Angie, I really don't know. I was young, still in high school. I read a lot and spent most of my time alone. I was good in school, I do know that; it was never hard for me.

"He came along and everything he liked I began to like. I don't know if I really liked it or if I just wanted to fit in with someone. He liked Heavy Metal music so I did too. I didn't like it before I met him or after we ended." A changed expression came over her face as if a light turned on for her. "It's weird. For the first time, sitting here, I'm beginning to realize it wasn't that great." She looked up at me. "Who was I in that relationship?"

"Who are you now?" I asked, wondering the same question about myself.

"Well, I know I don't like Heavy Metal and I never will, no matter what man I'm spending time with."

"But you'll be an object for any man who wants you to be?"

She glared at me. "I'm making a living!"

"Same thing," I said.

"What does that mean?"

"Who's paying you? Men!" I said. "You're not doing this for women, children or the elderly. You're doing it for dirty men who want nothing more from you than a hard on or an orgasm. It's just a form of prostitution. The men want it, so you give it. The women don't want it. The children don't want it. They're not paying you to do this." I thought for a moment. "What if all women stopped letting men objectify them, no participation in pornography, prostitution, strip bars? I'll tell you, there'd be an incredible change in all women's lives."

"It'll never happen," Rebecca said. "It's the young women that're into this. The older women are too smart. It works out perfectly for men. It's the young ones they want."

"No, they want whoever will let them treat them this way."

"I've never thought of it like that," she said.

"And maybe it's like how you were in that relationship. You wanted to fit in somewhere. You were young, maybe the young women just want to find a place where someone accepts them, and they know men will accept them if they're objects. They become wanted, desired, needed, loved, and liked, everything a young woman wants when she's trying to find herself."

She sat still, quietly staring into space.

"Anyway we got side tracked. I really want to know what your dreams were when you were younger."

"Well, Angie, I guess I've always wanted what most want. I wanted to meet a good man, get married, have lots of babies, and live happily ever after, white picket fence and all. I wanted to be a mother and wife."

"Really?" I had a hard time picturing it.

"Yes," she said with tears in her eyes.

The sincerity in her face allowed me to picture it clearly. "You're working in the wrong business if that's what you want."

"I know, and because of working there and what I've seen I'm not sure I could ever trust a man to be faithful. I hate men."

"There are good men out there," I said. "But not in your world. There are men out there who wouldn't set foot in a strip bar because they don't like what the women are doing with their lives."

"Yeah, how many, three?"

"No, Rebecca," I said seriously. "There are two."

She looked at me smiling from ear to ear, and we both started laughing.

"I can't believe you said that!" she said still giggling.

"Yes, I know. And the convenient thing about it is they're sitting right over there." I pointed to the two men still sitting at the bar. When she turned to look she laughed even harder because the men were turned around in their seats staring at the server's ass as she wiped off tables.

She rested her head on the table as she laughed silently.

Suddenly serious she said, "Why do I even want one. Sometimes I think when I'm older I'll get an older man, but then you have to deal with their mid-life crisis. So why even bother?"

"I don't know why we try so hard to make men love us," I said.

"It's not our fault, it's all around us. We have to look for red flags, look good, stay thin, smell good, act just right, play hard to get, be aggressive, be pure, be sexy, be innocent, be smart but not too smart, you have to stroke their egos. We have to keep sex alive. It's too much work. It has to be that bitch Cinderella," Rebecca said with a smile. "Except our fairy godmother is really a plastic surgeon."

I giggled at her wit.

"But maybe Cinderella was smart. Maybe she was running at midnight because she didn't want to be with him; maybe he was rude, and she saw the red flags about what her life would be like if she were with him. Maybe she didn't want the life he wanted for her; maybe she didn't want to lose her identity and become someone's wife. She wanted to be an artist. And when he came looking, she knew she was right about him. He was looking for a woman who didn't want to be found."

"Maybe the castle became her prison," I added.

Chapter 37

THE NEXT MORNING after taking Rebecca's car back to her, I caught the bus to the coffee shop where Veronica and I were meeting. I arrived early and took a table in the corner.

While I waited for Veronica, I remembered the first night I saw her dance. From the moment she walked out onto the stage, I could tell she was different from the other dancers in every way. Her body was hard, her breasts were small, and her dancing was powerful. She was not seductive; she was passionate. She danced with what seemed to be anger. Her dancing was strict, but her movements poetic. Her business was dancing, not seduction, like the others. She didn't smile; she was serious about what she was doing. I was surprised she kept her job, though she was the most entertaining to watch.

I looked up and Veronica was walking toward me dodging tables and chairs, trying not to spill her steaming coffee. She was wearing tan pants with a light blue denim shirt. Her dark skin, hair, and eyes were in brilliant contrast to the light blue she wore. Her skin was flawless, with no makeup that I could see, and her long wavy hair fell free.

"Hi, Angie. I'm not late, am I?" she asked.

"No, I was here early. Is this table OK with you?" I asked.

"It's fine. I'm going to get some ice. My coffee is too hot. I'll be right back. Do you want anything?"

"No, I'm fine," I said.

The place was busy. Three loud men in suits sat next to the door. There was an intriguing man, full of concentration, sitting alone at a back table. He was writing. His hair was black and pulled into a small tail in back. His widow's peak added to the vampire look that he was trying to achieve. He wore all black and a long black coat that looked like a cape. At another table two women sat across from each other holding hands under the table. A man and woman sat close to each other while whispering back and forth. A younger group of four sat in the center of the coffee shop, decorated with torn baggy clothes, face piercings and leather with chains. Each had a different color of hair: bright red, blue, orange, and a yellow and purple combination. I assumed they belonged to a group called rainbow, and green stayed home today.

"So, are we ready?" Veronica asked and sat down.

"Yes," I said. Because Veronica was different, I started my questioning differently. "What is it like working at The Gentlemen's Club?"

"You know people ask me that all the time, and I never really answer. It's hard to talk about. It's hard to work there. Don't get me wrong, it may not be hard for everybody. It's just hard for me.

"Then why do you work there?"

"It's the closest thing I can get to my dream right now."

"And your dream is?" I asked.

"Dancing! I love to dance. I love to entertain. I want to be an entertainer, not for men, but for people."

"Then why are you working there?"

"I'm doing what I love; I'm getting paid well. The downside is I'm naked and my audience is a bunch of perverted men."

"Is that the only downfall?"

"So far," she said. "I know what you're getting at, and you're right. It takes a toll on all of us. It's hard work, but for most of us it's worth it, at least for now. We all have our sad stories as to why we are there. To me, I'm better off than any of them."

"How do you mean?" I asked.

"I'm just fighting to get out of this place to get a better life. I deal with this shit every day so I can put money in the bank, and one day I'll be heading to New York to dance school. And that's when all this will be behind me," she said. Veronica looked up to the ceiling.

"I pray for that day. I've been poor my whole life; for the first time money is coming in. I help out my family when I can, I treat myself once in a while, and the rest goes toward my future."

"And what you have to do for a living, what you have to put up with, is worth it?" I questioned.

"I don't fit in; I don't play the part. You know from watching me, and I know you have been. Besides this is good school to life and men and to my dancing future. It can only get better."

"Do you have a boyfriend?"

"No, I've pretty much decided not to have a man in my life for many reasons. My dad's a jerk, he treats my mom and me like crap, and I have uncles who are the same way. Then working here, well, that's a whole other ball game," she said.

"Can you tell me about it?"

"Where should I start?"

"Let's say I'm your little sister, and I want to dance in a club like you. What advice would you give me?"

"Well, I feel like I know what I'm doing, and I think a lot of people who start working there don't know what they're getting into. So I wouldn't want my sister working in a place like this. It's too easy to get sucked in."

"Sucked into what?"

"Prostitution and drugs. I see it all the time. They come and go. The ones who don't get too involved stay awhile. But eventually they all get into some kind of trouble. How can you not get caught up in something when your self-esteem is this low to start with? These women get used, beat up, raped, drugged, and that's just the tip of the iceberg. You'd never know it by looking at the place. It looks like a nice classy place, right? 'Gentlemen's Club?' Wrong," she said and took a drink of her coffee. "Plus it looks like the bouncers protect these girls, right? Well they don't; they pimp them. And the dancers don't even know it. I stay out of it. I don't go to their parties. When my shift is over I go home. I rarely do table dances. I only do it to keep the bosses happy. I have a few regulars who have learned not to give me a hard time. I think it's charity, but I don't care. Honestly, I don't see what I do for them. I mean compared to these women, I'm built more like a man. Maybe that's what I do for them," she laughed.

"You said that's the tip of the iceberg, what else is there?"

"I've heard things, but I really can't say for sure. If I were more involved with this business, I'd know it all. I feel like an outsider. That's probably why I can see things more clearly than the other women. It's like I'm on the outside looking in."

She was different. Some of the others seemed in the middle of bullshit, Veronica wasn't. I could tell because I didn't even have to ask her what her goals and dreams were, she told me. And she hadn't lost sight of them over the years. "So you don't want a boyfriend or someone special in your life?"

"No. I don't have the time for a boyfriend, but I have lots of special people in my life."

"How did you become so strong?"

She laughed. "You should ask my mom. I know this sounds crazy, but she believes I'm a great aunt born again. I'm honestly flattered when she says it, and I've been hearing it my whole life, so I think that has made me feel different and special in some way."

"How did your aunt die?"

"Well, it was years and years ago. It's more like a family tale, but she was believed to be a witch, so they burned her at the stake. She just happened to be the most famous of us all," Veronica grinned. "I've done some reading on the subject and it's engrossing. It seems that usually witches were women rebelling. Women wanting things to be better for themselves, women who wouldn't go along with the norm. Women who wanted to create their own roads, not follow the roads already made. Women wanting a different religion. That's all, and they were burned and drowned for that, can you believe it?"

"Of course, it still happens today, not in the same way, but it happens."

"Leather" by Tori Amos was playing through the coffee shop. Veronica and I sat and listened. The song reminded me of all the women who sell themselves short. The piano and lyrics made me wish I could escape into her passion.

"That's a great song," I said.

"All her stuff is," Veronica said.

"Have you listened to Julie's CD?"

"No. Jody has it. She said it was really good."

"It is." I looked past her to the vampire. He had put his pen down and was just sitting there. "Should we go talk to the vampire?" I asked.

She turned around to look at him. "Sure."

I grabbed my tape recorder and notebook, stuffed them in my bag. I stood, grabbed my mocha and walked with her to his table.

"Hi! Do you mind if we join you for a minute?" Veronica asked.

"No, that's fine," he said, and he moved his notebook to keep us from reading it.

We grabbed two chairs and sat down. "So what are you writing about?" I asked.

"It's a short story about a lady friend of mine."

"Is she a vampire too?" I asked half jokingly.

Veronica turned her head to hide her laughter. I wasn't trying to be funny, and the vampire knew that.

"No, she's not, and neither am I, yet. Maybe one day," he said.

"So you want to be a vampire?" I asked.

"I want to live forever; I want to be immortal."

"Oh, well, that makes sense," I said. "So what's so great about life that makes you want to live forever?"

"Everything. The flowers, the seasons, this place, you," looking past me to the rainbow group, "them. All that surrounds me."

Veronica and I looked at each other then back to him. She said, "If you're serious, you're brilliant!" and she meant it.

"Thank you," he said. "I'm Trayn."

"I'm Veronica."

"And I'm Angie." We didn't shake hands; we just nodded to each other.

"Angie. You intrigue me," he said.

"Well, vampi…Trayn," I smiled. "You intrigue me, too. So you come here often?" I asked.

"Yes, I do." He looked right into my eyes and said, "I'd like to paint you. I write, but I paint by nature."

"I paint but write by nature," I said.

"Are you in a gallery?" Veronica asked.

"Yes, I'm at Second and Cedar: Verk Art Gallery."

"Really? Wow!" Veronica said. "I'd love to see your work."

"We could head over there now if you want," Trayn said.

Veronica looked at me.

"We can finish later. Should we go?" I asked.

"Yeah, let's go," she said and stood up. "Let's walk, it's only a few blocks."

Trayn and I stood, and we all headed to the door.

Trayn had about a dozen pieces on display plus one in the front window. I couldn't understand how such a lover of life could paint such pain. Every color he used was mixed with black. In some you could make out a body image with no real form, like his shadow hiding in the corner of his mind running from the light. I felt sorrow looking at his work. I couldn't understand it, but I could feel it. I felt a connection with him I couldn't explain. I was looking at his soul. When I turned to face him, he saw my sensitivity to his work.

Trayn said, "Thank you" with sincerity in his eyes.

Veronica loved his work, but I knew she didn't feel it to the same extent. I sensed she believed there was an attraction between Trayn and me.

"You know this gallery is kind of off the wall. Do you want to look around a while? There's an upstairs too," Trayn said to Veronica. Then, to me, he said, "It's the only gallery that would take me."

I wanted to do a piece on him and his work. I wanted to help promote him. He was good. I took down his name and number before we left. Veronica and I headed toward a restaurant by the coffee shop.

"You love his work, don't you?"

"Yes, I do," I said. "Why am I so lucky to be surrounded by such talented people. Julie and her music, now Trayn with his painting, and you.

"What do you mean me?" she asked smiling.

"Well, not only do you seem to have your head on straighter than me, your dancing is awesome. And I agree with you. I don't know why you still have your job. Anyone can see you're not there to fulfill men's fantasies. It's different for you," I said. "But still, isn't it hard on you?"

"Of course, but I'm telling you, there is no other way for me. I'm from a poor family. I didn't graduate from high school. This is all I have. Because of this place I was able to get my GED. I figure about six more months of this, and I'll be on my way to New York. And that's what keeps me going. It's all I have, Angie."

"I'm sad for some of the other women who work at the club, but I'm not sad for you. You're going to make it."

"I'm sad for some of those women, too," she said. "A lot of them can't see past the club. Maybe that's when we die inside, when we can't see the light ahead, or we have nothing left to fight for."

Veronica and I talked for hours over lunch. She seemed to know what she wanted and how she would get it. But as strong as she seemed, she was still in a place where she was kept down and degraded.

Chapter 38

I CALLED TRAYN the next day. I think he expected my call. Yesterday in the gallery I wanted to talk to him alone, and I think both he and Veronica sensed that.

"I just caught up on some of your stuff," Trayn said.

"Really?" I was flattered.

"I really like what you do. More men should read it," he said.

"Thanks, I wish more would," I said. "So do you want to get together? I'd like to talk about your work."

"You're not interested in my painting. You're interested in me," he teased.

"Maybe, but not in the way you'd want me to be."

He laughed and said, "I'd love to meet you. How do you feel about Guthery Park?"

"That sounds great. One o'clock?" I asked.

"Sure. Dress warm, it's a chilly one," he said and hung up the phone.

He was a half-an-hour late, wearing his black cape coat. I should have known. Time doesn't mean a lot to the artist. I was glad he didn't have an excuse, just "Sorry, I'm late."

We walked around in the cool breeze, looked at the sculptures, and talked. He told me about the roadblocks he had to face with his art and how when they had piled up, blocked him in, he started writing. Initially he had journaled his frustrations, but he soon discovered writing was another love.

That night I was planning to work on my article, but when Trayn invited me to his place to see some of his other work, I accepted. I wanted to talk to him more, he was so interesting, and I felt our connection was worth more time.

I explored his paint scented studio, trying to find something to explain his art. There was nothing but more art with that same pain showing so clearly. There were two different types of his work. He said it was a before and after he found out the truth of his family. I wanted to know more but didn't press it.

"My mother shot my father," Trayn suddenly said. "I was thirteen."

I turned around, and he was sitting on a barstool covered with dried paint. His head was down but not for sympathy. He was surprised he was telling me. He raised his head. His face was blank from emotion except his eyes. The outer corners drooped and his lids lowered slightly. "I was there. I saw her do it."

"I had stayed home from school that day. I wasn't sick. I just didn't want to go, and Mom let me stay home. I was on the couch watching TV. The living room was completely blocked from the kitchen, but I could hear my mother making me lunch.

"There was a knock at the door, and my mom went to answer it. Before she got to it, I heard the door fly open. My mom screamed. I hid behind the couch. I could hear him punching her and her body hitting the floor. I remember her screaming 'Trayn's home, Trayn's home!' I was scared and didn't know what was happening, I was too afraid to look. He kept knocking her down, then kicking her. She kept screaming 'Don't! Trayn's home! Please! Trayn! Please!' He kept kicking her.

"I found some bravery and crawled out from behind the couch toward the kitchen to fight the monster. That's when I saw my dad. I thought he was there to save us, but he was walking toward the door. I didn't understand. Then I heard a loud bang. I fell to the ground as I saw my father go down. I turned to my mother in time to see her expression of fear. She dropped the gun, and I ran out of the house. I never went back.

"I always thought the fear in her eyes was from shooting the wrong man. I later learned it was because I saw it happen. Years later, my grandmother found me to tell me my mother was dying of cancer. I went to the hospital to see her. And that's when I found out the truth.

"My mother took the abuse for years. She hid it well. She had been spending time at the women's shelter and was going through with a divorce from my dad. They were separated for some time, but he was unemployed and sometimes needed a place to stay. One day while I was at school my father beat her so badly she spent a week in the hospital. My grandmother was at the house when I got home from school. She told me my mom and dad went on a little vacation and would be home next week. My dad was really in jail. While my mom was in the hospital, she got an order for protection, and her brother gave her a gun and a run down on using it.

"It happened the day he got out of jail. That's the day she killed him. My mother told me that day in the hospital. I remember crying hard and I yelled at her, 'Mom you shot him in the back! He was leaving! You killed him while he was walking away!' I stood to look down at her and continued screaming at her. 'You're a fucking bitch and I hate you! I hate you for what you did to him. He was my father! I will never forgive you! I hope you go straight to hell and burn! You had no right taking my father away from me!'

"In her weakened raspy voice she said to me, 'Oh, God, Trayn… Your father wasn't walking away… he was just going to close the door. He was going to kill me. Before he went for the door he had knelt down next to me and held my chin as he spoke. He squeezed so hard with just his bare hand that he pressed out three of my back teeth. I was crying in pain for him to stop. He lowered his face next to mine and kissed my cheek. He told me not to worry the pain would end soon, it was my last day, and that's when he let go of me and went to close the door. I thought you'd be better off with me… but I lost you anyway.' She told me she'd always loved me and always put me first. She said I meant more to her than anything.

"I was crying. I didn't believe her or didn't want to. I got up and left the room. Out in the hall, my grandmother was sitting on a bench crying. She'd heard all that was said. I stared at her for the truth.

"She said it was true and put her head back down. I wondered why nobody had told me and asked it out loud. My grandma said they tried, but I wouldn't listen. She said I was young and looked up to my father. They thought it was time I knew the truth so I could make peace with my mother before she passed away.

"It had all been a lie. My life was a lie! He was going to kill my mom! My dad was going to kill my mom! I couldn't believe it. I collapsed on the floor as the full realization began to sink in. Hot bitter tears streamed down my face as I crawled on my hands and knees back into my mom's room. When I got to the bed I stood and reached for her. I lifted her upper body in my arms to wake her. I held her, rocking her, crying, telling her I loved her. I loosened my hold on her to look into her eyes but she was gone.

"My grandmother walked into the room and stood behind me. She kissed the back of my head and whispered, 'She knows.'

"If it hadn't been for my grandmother I wouldn't have made it," Trayn said to me. "You can see the difference in my work so clearly. My first work was hatred toward my mother and women. Now it's hatred toward my father, men and me. I'm working toward forgiveness, that's this over here," he said, walking toward a more colorful painting off by itself.

"I like forgiveness!" I said. "With forgiveness you may find fewer roadblocks, too."

"Touché," he said and smiled.

I smiled back.

Chapter 39

I WENT TO Bonnie's apartment the next day to interview her. Originally we were to meet in the morning, but she called and said something came up so she wanted to change it to the evening. When I arrived, an eleven-year-old girl, Holly, was there.

"Angie, can I talk to you for a minute?" Bonnie asked.

"Sure," I said, and we headed for the kitchen leaving Holly on the couch in the living room.

Bonnie faced me. "Angie, Holly's my little sister, and her mother'll be here in a few minutes to pick her up."

Bonnie was close to my age, her blondish brown hair was layered long and the color perfectly matched the mole on her upper lip. "Are you in the little sister/big sister program?" I asked.

"Yes, I am, and they don't know what I do for a living, so please don't say anything. I'll introduce you as one of my friends."

I agreed. "That's fine, but didn't they do a background check before they... "

"I lied about everything and got away with it," she interrupted. "Please don't give it away. Holly needs me right now."

"OK," I agreed, feeling concerned that someone could lie their way into a position of dealing with children.

We walked back into the living room just as there was a knock on the door. Holly's mom didn't wait for "come in." She walked in and headed straight for Holly. It was obvious they were related. They had the same blond hair, fair skin, and big brown eyes.

"Hi, Baby. How was your day? Did you and Bonnie have fun?" she asked and gave Holly a big hug.

Holly answered, "Yeah."

I wondered how Holly's mom would feel if she knew what Bonnie really did for a living.

"Well, we have a big night planned don't we honey?" She turned to Bonnie. "I promised her she could bake cookies tonight alone. The two of you have baked cookies so much together, so she feels she's had plenty of practice and tonight's the night. But first we're going to rent a couple movies." She turned to Holly helping her with her jacket and pulling her long hair from beneath it. "You have everything?"

"What kind of cookies are you making?" I asked Holly.

"Chocolate chip."

Bonnie said, "Oh, I'm sorry. This is one of my good friends, Angie. Angie, this is Holly's mom, Mary."

We shook hands. "Well, honey, we better get goin'," Mary said. "It was nice to meet you."

"It was nice to meet you, too. And it was nice to meet you, Holly. Have fun with the cookies."

They were walking out the door. Holly yelled, "Bye."

Bonnie said, "I'll see you next weekend," before she closed the door.

"I can't believe you have a little sister, Bonnie," I said trying to sound happy about it, but I wasn't.

"She's a special little girl, Angie. Should we go into the kitchen?" She said as if trying to change the subject. "We can sit at the table." We started walking that way. "Do you want anything to drink?" she asked. "I have pop, water, I could make some coffee or, oh, I have iced tea," she said as she opened the refrigerator door.

"Some iced tea would be great," I said. "How long have you been in the big sister/little sister program?"

"Holly and I have been together for about a year." She handed me my drink and sat down.

"Have you been working at the club that long?" I asked.

"It was about the same time I started working there. Then I had more money, and more time, so I got into the program. I'm not sure how, but I'm thankful."

"I know sometimes the kids in the program have problems. Is Holly doing OK?"

"Well, it depends on what you call OK," she said. "I'd say, any kid who's gone through what she's gone through isn't OK and never really will be. I should know."

"What do you mean?" I asked.

"She was molested by her stepfather."

I slowly shook my head in disbelief. "I can't believe this. Everywhere I go, every time I turn around there's some sick shit hurting a woman or child. I'm so tired of it!" I said.

"I know, you're right," she said. "I'm sure you see a lot of it being a writer for a women's paper."

"Yes, I do," I said. "How is Holly doing?"

"Oh, she is so bright and wonderful. She's doing good, but she's always going to have problems. I hope I'm helping."

"I'm sure you are," I said. I noticed how Bonnie's nails had been bitten so short that they had to hurt. "You have a habit there."

"Yeah. Ever since I was young."

"Did it happen to you, too?" I asked.

"No, but I've read a lot about it. One book I read pushed me into wanting to help children that've been through this type of abuse."

"What was the book about?" I asked.

"A little girl lost her mother in a car accident, and her father kind of went crazy and started abusing her."

"Wow. Like the girl didn't have enough to deal with losing her mother."

"I know. Most men are weak and broken. They are so susceptible to abusing, crime, and all the bullshit in this society," she said. "And it only robs them and the people in their lives. It's twisted."

"From my travels I've found many more men abusing drugs and alcohol than women."

"Plus, I bet the women who do get hooked on drugs and alcohol first start because a man got them to try it."

"I wonder," I said. I began thinking about women in prisons, and I wondered why they were there. A good friend worked as an advocate to help prostitutes find a better life. He also worked to help the women in prisons. He always told me that 99 percent of the women in prisons had been molested as children. And 100 percent of the prostitutes had been.

"How a man's empty promises led them to do things they knew were wrong," she added.

"If you feel so strongly about this, why do you work where you work?" I asked.

"I know, I'm part of the problem," she said and put the tips of her fingers to her mouth and started biting for a second. "But I'm able to go to school, and I have time to study. I make good grades."

"What are you going to school for?" I asked.

"Psychology," she said. "Specializing in child abuse."

"I think there is one thing you should think about if you really want to help children in the future. You have to understand that if they ever do a background check and find out you've been lying and what you do for a living, you may never get into that line of work no matter how good your grades are."

"There's no other way for me," she said.

"Bonnie, now *you're* being weak. There's always another way," I said.

Bonnie stood, grabbed her glass, and walked over to the sink. She dumped her ice out and set the glass on the counter. She turned around. "You're right, and I knew it the day I started working there," she said leaning against the counter. "I don't know how to fix it."

"I can help if you want."

"I just don't want to lose Holly or my future."

"We'll work it out," I said.

Bonnie and I spent about five hours together. In that time, she became more open about her own past, and she became my friend. We made chocolate chip cookies, we cried, we laughed, and we cried again after eating most of the cookies.

Chapter 40

THE ARTICLE WAS out, and Julie and I went to the club to say goodbye to our new friends. We tried to make it fun, but we were all a little sad that it was over. That night, I jokingly mentioned we should take the club over and make the men dance so they would know what it felt like to be humiliated. We giggled imagining it.

Throughout this experience with these women, I hoped I had made a difference in their lives. I wasn't sure, but it seemed they were feeling differently about their lifestyles and some of the dancers even started looking for other work.

Julie and I invited the women I had interviewed to Julie's house for a little get together to brainstorm on finding a way out of the sex industry. It was also a way to hang onto my new friends a little longer.

I walked toward the bathroom. The eyes of the men in the club followed me every step of the way. It sickened me. I was not there to be looked at, but they all thought it was OK because I *was* there. As I approached the bathroom, I noticed a Spanish-speaking man using the pay phone on the wall. He seemed to be the only man who didn't acknowledge me.

I entered the bathroom and Sara was fixing her hair in front of the sink. Surprisingly, she smiled at me from the mirror.

I smiled back and said, "Hi, how are you doing tonight?"

She turned toward me and said, "I hear you're having a party next weekend."

"Well, it's not really a party, just a little get together. You're invited, you know."

"Really?" she said.

"Of course."

"Should I bring something?"

"Well, if you want to bring something you can, but you don't have to. Julie and I aren't drinkers, so if you'd like something special to drink you might want to bring that."

"Thanks, Angie. Well, I better get back," she said as she headed to the door.

"I really hope to see you there, Sara, it should be a nice time," I said.

"You will," she said. The door closed behind her.

Chapter 41

THE PARTY WAS to start in an hour. Julie and I had been cleaning, rearranging her house. We had gone to the store earlier to purchase chips, crackers, and pop. We decided not to supply alcohol for the party, so we skipped the liquor store.

Everything was ready. We sat down in her living room to relax, both with a can of pop. Just as Julie sat down the phone rang. She moaned and got up to answer it. I reached to the wrought iron and glass end table to take a drink of my diet coke.

Her house was old with lots of character. She hadn't lived there long but she'd bought a lot of beautiful furniture. Though it was only a one bedroom, every room was large. The kitchen, dining area had so much space, even with her table and eight chairs in it. Not only was Julie good with music, she did a great job decorating and remodeling. With each new thing I learned about Julie, I admired her more.

Julie walked out of the kitchen and stood in the hall with her hands on her hips, staring at me with a dumbfounded grin on her face. "That was the call I've been waiting for," she said.

"What call?" I asked.

She smiled and walked into the living room, "Angie, we're going on tour!"

I stood up. "You're kidding? When? Where? For how long?"

She started laughing and said, "My God, you are a reporter."

We hugged. "This is it, Julie! You're on your way! I'm so happy for you!"

"Thanks," she said and broke our hug to face me. "You helped me get here. You've helped me in so many ways. Oh, Angie, what would I ever do without you?"

"Sounds like you'll be without me for a while," I said. I was excited for her, but sad, too.

"No, I won't. You're always with me," she said and placed her hand on her heart. "Besides that, there is stuff to write about everywhere you go, and if you can ever get away, I want you to join me. For a week, a month, or even just a day if you can."

"I know! I'll join you for your whole tour. I'll follow you around with my tape recorder and notebook. I'll write a book all about you, your whole life story that you're so secretive about," I teased. "I bet it would be a best seller."

"No, best in the cellar. I'm not secretive, it's just the past is the past— it deserves to be laid to rest. It takes too much energy remembering it all, carrying it all."

"Getting all philosophical on me? Don't you have a song about that anyway?"

She gently punched me in the arm. "You think you're so cute."

"Just don't forget. I do listen to your CD. I do listen to your words. You're good, but my song is the best one on it," I said punching her back.

She grabbed her shoulder as if I hurt her. Then after seeing my expression she let go and started laughing. "You're right it's good, even if nobody else thinks so," she joked. "Anyway, it sounds like we'll be gone for about three months to start with. We'll have a short break, see how things are going, and if all is well, then we'll hit the road again. We'll be leaving in about a month or so. I'll know more next week," she said. "And I'm serious. I want you to join me whenever you can. Remember the fun we had traveling?"

"How could I forget? It was the best time of my life, my best friend by my side, and total freedom."

"Yeah, we had some great times."

"The best!"

"That's why you have to join me on the road," she demanded.

"I'd love to. I'll come later on, after you've gotten used to it all."

"That's probably a good idea. I have an idea what to expect from the local touring we've done, but this is different. I'm so excited!"

"Call Tammy and Barb. What are you waiting for?"

"I want to tell them in person. Barb should be here soon. I should call Tammy though."

"Call her!"

"OK." She went back into the kitchen.

I returned to the living room and sat down. I couldn't believe it. Julie was really on her way straight to the top. I knew she had what it takes. I thought, maybe I should write a book. Maybe I should aim higher, but I'm happy where I am, considering where I've been.

There was a knock at the door. I yelled, "Come in!" I figured it would be Barb, but it was Jody.

"Hi, Angie. I came early to talk to you about something," she said and closed the door behind her. "Do you have a minute?" she asked.

"Sure have a seat. Do you want anything to drink? We have a lot of pop."

"No. I'm fine." She sat down, "I've been thinking about something you said and I want to run it by you."

"OK."

"Remember that day you were at the club talking to Rebecca and you mentioned all of us opening a business? Well, I have some ideas."

"Really? That's wonderful," I said. "Let's hear them."

"OK. The first one, well, I thought we could open a flower shop. There is an old lady who lives by me who's retiring and selling her shop. It's been there for fifteen years. It's small but seems to keep busy. It's in a good location. I thought this would be nice for us because of the different environment. Instead of spreading sex and lust, we'd be sending love and happiness."

I was excited. "Jody, that sounds like a great idea. You would all get such good feelings out of it. Have you talked to any of the others?" I asked.

"No. But I have another idea. I'd heard of some women who started a shuttle service for kids, and I thought we could get some vans and start something like that. We all love kids. And I know being around kids would be a lift for all of us compared to what we're doing now. We'd be helping families, instead of sick men getting off."

"Wow! Jody you have been thinking. I'm not sure about the shuttle service."

"Because of where we work, huh?"

I nodded. "But I love the flower shop idea."

"I've done some research. I have figures. I know what she pays in rent and what she made last year. If enough of us are interested, we could find another flower shop or something else completely. I'll do anything."

"You really want out, don't you?"

"Yes, I do."

"Congratulations, Jody, I'm so proud of you!"

"Thanks, Angie, but I can't do it alone. How do I get the others to come with me?"

"That's one of the reasons we're all meeting. Jody, you're well liked by everybody. If you talk to them about this, show them the research you've done, they'll know you're serious. Besides, everybody coming here tonight wants out," I said. "I'd start by talking to Bonnie."

"Really?"

Barb, Julie's bass player, walked in the front door. "Hey," she said. "I'm just here to grab a CD from Julie."

I just sat there pointing to the kitchen.

"What?" she asked.

"Just go into the kitchen," I said smiling.

She knew something was up, so she grinned and headed that way. I stood up and motioned for Jody to come along. We followed her to the doorway and stood there.

Julie saw Barb and put the phone down. "Barb! We got it!" Julie stood and hugged her.

"Got what?" Barb asked. "What's up?"

"We're going on tour!"

Barb started crying. "No, we're not!"

"Yes, we are!"

"When?" she screamed. Before she let Julie answer she pointed to the phone. "Is that Tammy?" she asked and picked it up. "Tammy!"

Julie walked over to me and we hugged again, this time including Jody, then Barb, with phone in hand, joined our group hug full of giggles, happy screams, and tears.

Chapter 42
The Gentlewomen's Club

RIGHT AFTER BARB left with the CD, Bonnie, Veronica and Rebecca showed up. We sat in the living room, and Jody began to tell the others about the flower shop idea.

Rebecca interrupted. "Kay went and got implants."

"That is so dumb!" Julie exploded.

We all laughed at her enthusiasm.

"Her natural breasts didn't work?" Julie asked sarcastically. "Do you know what your breasts are for? To feed babies and for sexual stimulation; I bet hers worked just fine. Think about that, if you enlarge them for any reason it's to be more attractive to pig men." Julie shook her head in frustration. "Besides, we birth their babies and lug them around for years. Then they like large breasts so we mutilate our bodies with implants and lug breasts around for men. No thank you!"

"Guys would never do that shit for us," Veronica said. "And I respect them for it. Let's run around and ask our men to pierce their penises because it would be more stimulating for us. They would look at us like we've gone mad. I wish more women would have looked at men and said, "You're fuckin' crazy if you think I'd do that for you! But we start feeling insecure like we're not stacking up, literally."

"If it ain't broke don't fix it," Jody said, ready to get to the flower shop talk.

"I don't even like to be looked at by men. I like to look nice, for me. But I hate to be looked at in that way, you know, that way," Veronica said.

The others nodded.

"One of the first things I had published was a quote I had printed on a T-shirt. I wrote, 'I feel angry when men look at me.' Somebody saw it and put it in an article on abuse against women. I was proud." I smiled. "But you know, sometimes I wish I could just be out there, dress a little sexy, get that type of attention and be OK with it, but I'm not."

"I remember a time," Bonnie said, "before I was a dancer. I went to this cafeteria at this, well it was a community building, and it was connected to a mall. I was so hungry I couldn't wait to get some good food in me. The place wasn't very busy, so when I walked in I noticed four guys serving the food. They stood in a huddle and all stared at me, smiling and eyeing me, laughing among themselves. I was so uncomfortable, I didn't—I couldn't— even approach the counter. I immediately turned to the fountain pop counter, got a diet seven-up, and headed to the cashier. By the register were some rice crispy bars, so that's what I ate instead of the meal I really needed. And as I sat at my table eating, I noticed a couple of them were taking a break. They stared down every woman who walked by. It made me angry, and I could tell the women knew it was going on and it made them uncomfortable. And another thing, these women were dressed in suits. They weren't wearing miniskirts, short shorts, or low-cut blouses. Some were covered from neck to wrist to ankle."

"Yeah, wouldn't it be nice if a man could approach a couple of men staring at a woman, and tell them to knock it off. Or say, isn't it sad, it's really too bad she feels she has to dress that way, showing her body like it's a piece of meat. It would make those guys think twice," Veronica declared.

"Or they'd just call him a pussy or a queer," Julie said. "If she dresses all loose, men come along, point at her, and make jokes, lowering them- selves to her level of insecurities."

Chapter 43

SARA WALKED IN. "Hi."

I could see the intimidation on her face, so I jumped up to greet her. I gave her a hug and told her I was happy she made it.

"Am I late?"

"No," Jody said. "We were just going to talk about the possibilities of joining together and buying a flower shop."

"Wow! That sounds great," Sara said and sat next to me on the love seat.

It didn't take long for the conversation to switch again. Julie began talking about moments in life that cause you to go down a completely different road, an unexpected turn that changes your life forever.

Jody was suddenly serious. "All right, I'll tell you one of mine." After a deep breath she said, "I was raped."

Everyone went silent. Rebecca and I shared a look, and Jody continued. "It was a man I knew. In fact, I had a serious crush on him. I tried to spend time with him, hoping he'd notice me. One night I asked him for a ride home, and then he did notice me. He opened the car door for me and I slid in. I leaned over, unlocked and opened his door. When he got in he gave me a smile.

"He asked me what I'd like to listen to on the stereo and suggested Madonna. I remember looking out the window at the passing homes. He was kinder to me than I thought he'd be. I wondered what his house looked like.

"He told me he had left his checkbook at home and had to get gas before work the next day. He asked if I minded stopping off at his place first and said it would only take a second. It was just around the corner. We pulled into the driveway and he got out. He poked his head back in and asked if I wanted to come in. He said he was kind of a slob and it might take him a minute to find it. I accepted and started to think that maybe he liked me too.

"I sat on his couch and he joined me. It was nice and cool in his house, and he didn't want to leave yet. That's when he tried to kiss me. I could smell alcohol on his breath. Before I knew what was happening he was on top of me, touching me. He was too heavy to get off. I didn't understand what was happening. I'd budge and shift beneath him trying to get away, but I couldn't. He wouldn't let me; his hold was too tight. I started to cry, begging him to stop, but it only made him more aggressive.

"He pulled at my shorts, trying to remove them. I had one hand holding on to them, keeping them in place. He lifted my shirt and bra with one swift move of his hand. I reached to pull my blouse back down, and he yanked my shorts off and pulled my panties to the side, ripping them. He held my hands over my head as he tried to thrust inside me. My heels were planted on the floor giving me just enough leverage to move back, matching the timing of his attempt to enter me. I got tired and my hair was stuck under my back. With the last of my lunges back, I could feel my hair being pulled from my head. The harder I fought, the harder he tried. But I kept fighting, until… he punched me." Jody was still and expressionless almost as if she were watching the whole experience over again, but it was happening to someone else.

"He hit me in the face so hard my body went limp. That's when it happened." She raised her hand and wiped her tears away, then continued.

"After he came, he was on top of me for a while. I just lay there and cried. I couldn't believe what had happened. I'd been raped! I tried to get out from underneath him, and he asked me, "Where you goin', Hon?"

I said, "Get off me!" while trying to push him off.

"What's wrong?" he asked.

My face was swollen with blood running out of my nose, and I cried, "You raped me!"

He got up, adjusted his pants saying, "Oh, sure! You fuckin' bitch!" He grabbed my shorts and threw them at me, "Get the fuck out of here, you fuckin' slut!"

Veronica sitting next to her with tears in her eyes, asked, "Did he go to jail?"

"Yes, he finally did, but it was a long process, and it was really hard on me. After I left his place I kept replaying the night through my head. I thought that maybe I'd asked for it in some way without knowing it. Were my shorts too short? Was I flirting too much? By going into his home, did I tell him I'd have sex with him? When I got home I called the rape hotline and talked to a counselor about what'd happened. I knew not to take a shower, but I wasn't sure what to do. He'd made me feel like I had asked for it. So I thought it was my fault. The counselor convinced me to go to the hospital to get checked. That's the best thing I could've done.

"A woman from the hot line met me there. She stayed with me through the whole thing. My body became a crime scene. The doctors took pictures and got evidence, pubic hair and semen. At that point, I was stuck on pressing charges; going to court scared me. I took it one step at a time. I got a lot of help from the hotline and counselors. Later I found out I wasn't the only one. The other woman and I decided to press charges, and we put him away.

"When it was over, we both wanted to talk to each other, so we met. We became friends. She lives about a hundred miles away, but we get together when we can. It's amazing how something so bad can make a friendship so good. She's one of my best friends. There was one other woman, but she wouldn't come forward."

I was surprised Jody was being so open with us, but it brought the whole group closer. We let our guard down, and Jody opened the door for all of us to have a much deeper connection.

"My life will never be the same. That's when my road suddenly turned. Trusting a man has always been hard, but now it's almost impossible. I'm scared every day, all night, and every place I go."

"God, I'm so sorry," Rebecca said.

"You know the way he made you feel, like it was your fault? I think a lot of guys do that, make us think when they do something wrong, something that hurts us, it's our fault. It's always our fault. We're not good enough mothers, daughters, and especially not good enough wives. Women get blamed for everything," Julie added. "I think it all started when we convinced Adam to eat the apple."

"Angie? What was your turning point?"

"I don't know. I've had many. I'm beginning to realize my issues with men. I think it started when my father left the family. Then my mother had a lot of men around, but none of them stayed. I think I always wanted a dad. I don't know anything about men; I mean I never had a permanent male figure in my life. It's hard for me to trust and understand what having a partner for life would mean. But deep down I still want a good man in my life. I just hope when he comes along, he will be patient with me." I said.

"If he's going to be with you, he'll have to be patient." Julie said, with a grin on her face. "Not a big enough turn, Ang. We'll give you another chance later."

I smiled back as some of the girls started laughing.

"Part of my problem was *having* my father in my life. That did it for me," Jody said and reached for her bottle of water on the coffee table. "I would have to hear things from my dad like, 'I went to the doctor the other day, and I ended up with a female doctor. I just didn't trust her. I don't think she knows what she's talking about. For God's sake, she's a woman, not a doctor!' Or, my brother and I would be in the car with him and he'd say to my brother, 'Look at that woman, she is so ugly, I wouldn't fuck her with your dick. Ha ha ha,' they'd laugh right in front of me." She took a drink. "Or 'Your grades don't matter honey, you just look pretty so you can get married like your mother did and your husband will take care of you.'

"One time I was seeing a guy that my dad just loved. He had—well, his family had—a lot of money. He came to our house to pick me up for our date. I actually heard my father say to him, 'If she gives you any trouble let me know.' Like I was a car he just sold him! So as you can see, my dad put me in my place for eighteen years of my life."

"No wonder you thought it was your fault when you were raped," Julie said.

"Bingo," Jody said. "For about the past year things have really changed for me. I've been getting help, and I'm trying to put the old way of thinking behind me. Most of my life I've spent as a walking, talking blowup doll for men. I still struggle, but I know now I'm worth more than just being a prize for men."

"And still you work where you work," Julie said.

"I will tell you one thing: knowing you two," she said looking at me and Julie, "has changed my life more in the past couple weeks than one year of therapy. My shrink's been trying to get me out of that club for months. Now I'm finally leaving. I feel great about it."

Julie walked over and gave Jody a hug.

Chapter 44

"OK, VERONICA, YOUR turn."

"Hmm, let's see… life changing." She said looking up, searching, smiling hesitantly. Then suddenly serious. "I had an abortion. I was in love with a man for about eight months and became pregnant. The stress of the baby caused us to fight. I wasn't ready to have a baby and, emotionally, neither was he. Because I knew I'd probably end up alone raising the child, I considered abortion. When he realized I believed in abortion, he completely ended the relationship. So I went through with it. It was hard, but I'm glad I did it. I wasn't ready for motherhood, especially without the fatherhood."

"I don't know about that," Bonnie said.

"Well, why is my life any less important than the baby's or his. Because I'm a woman? I mean, he didn't want the baby, but he didn't want me to have an abortion either. So I had to make a decision and that was it. Oh, and about three months after my abortion, he tried to get back into my life. Like, 'The pressure's off, I want you back.' Get real!"

"Boy, abortion is a touchy subject. I've never been put in that situation, but I don't think I could do it. That's a life inside. I couldn't live with that decision," Bonnie said.

"Amy was put in a similar situation, but she chose to have the baby. Now she works in a strip club to support her. She didn't get to finish college, the father isn't around and doesn't pay child support. She's always envious of women without children," Jody told us.

"The only thing I've changed is I'm more careful with who I choose to sleep with, just in case. I have to know a man *so* well before I sleep with him. I have to know that if I got pregnant he'd stick around, be dependable, marry me, and treat me right!" Veronica said. "My new rule is I date a man for about three to four months before we make love. If it doesn't last that long, it wouldn't last a pregnancy, so it doesn't matter."

"That's a really good way of looking at it," I said.

"Yes, but it really gets lonely. I've only had one lover in the past year and a half, and he only lasted about eight months."

"I'm not judging Amy or putting her down. She's not here to defend herself. I've met her little girl and she's an angel, but what message is she giving her daughter? If things get hard, become a stripper? Sell yourself?" Julie asked.

"Julie, she started looking for a new job Monday, and yesterday she checked into going back to school and getting financial help. Things are looking good for her," Veronica explained.

"She's getting out, too? That's great. I had no idea," Julie said.

"What is an abortion like anyway?" Bonnie asked.

"Well, it's...it's hard to explain. I'll tell you about my situation. I drove to the place. When I was walking to the building I feared being shot. The fear followed me in the elevator and in the halls until I was in the office. I told them my name. They gave me forms to fill out and told me to sit in the waiting room. There were so many women, and most were not alone. Some had friends with them and others had their boyfriends along for support. They were from all walks of life, rich, poor, young and old.

"I was called into a room where they took blood and urine samples. Then I went back out to the waiting room. Next, I was called back into a counselor's office where I paid her three hundred dollars. The woman asked if I was sure this was what I wanted. I was sure. So it was back to the waiting room. I went into another room to watch a film on what I could expect and what the doctor would be doing. I was then called back into a room where they did an ultrasound. There I was informed that the fetus was only about five weeks old and they may not be able to do the abortion. They said they could try, but I'd have to come back again if it was unsuccessful. I said that would be fine. I had gone in early on purpose because I felt it would be easier, convincing myself that a new life hadn't started yet. They normally didn't perform abortions until the fetus was around eight weeks old.

"So I moved into another room and was tested for STDs. That was my choice. Whatever they were able to check there came back negative. Back to the waiting room to wait for my turn. Three at a time were called, and we went off to the other waiting room, where we removed all our clothing, waist down. It was my turn to go in. A nurse walked with me, and I got up on the table like I was getting a Pap smear, and waited. Another nurse came in and got me ready, opened me up with a speculum. The doctor came in and gave me a shot inside my vagina. Then I was told I'd feel some cramping, and he started the vacuum inside of me. It was fine until I realized what was going on and right then, there were problems. I felt nauseous but it wasn't because of the pain, which wasn't that bad. It was because of what I was doing. I was killing my little baby.

"I heard the nurse say, 'Something's not right. Veronica, sit up a little bit.'

"The doctor was done and left the room. The nurse suddenly began yelling out the door, 'I need another nurse in here right away!' The nurse told me to lie back down and relax. Then she opened the door again and yelled, 'Can someone get me a glass of water?'

"The other nurse came in and asked, 'Is she losing a lot of blood?'

"'No, it's something else.'

"The second nurse started taking my blood pressure and pulse. She said, 'Keep her still until her blood pressure elevates! I'll be right back.'

"What's wrong?" I asked.

"She said, 'You'll be fine. You just lost a lot of color, and your blood pressure dropped pretty low. Here, why don't you try some water?'

"A few minutes later the second nurse came back in. 'How's she doing?'

"'Better.'

"They helped me up and into a private recovery room, separate from all the other women. They told me I couldn't leave until I had a ride home, which I didn't. So they kept me for about an hour and forty-five minutes, when most women could leave after only thirty minutes. They kept checking my pulse and blood pressure until they felt I was OK and could drive home on my own. I left feeling relieved yet sad in a way. Now, I just try not to think about it," Veronica said.

"Ya know," Julie said, "That whole birth control thing really bugs me. If I'm going to be with a man there is no question, a condom will be used. I don't care if we've dated one month or one year. One reason is to protect myself from disease. Another reason is to protect me from pregnancy. The most important reason is I will not use a birth control which might give me side effects, headaches, weight gain, irregular bleeding, depression, abdominal pain, blood clots, heart attack, stroke, increase in cramps… my God."

I started laughing. "You certainly have those memorized," I teased.

"Condoms really don't fuck with my body, they protect it. Besides, it's the only birth control method that is the man's responsibility. Yet it doesn't hurt either one of us physically. Women have enough to worry about with our periods, pregnancy, and an abortion if there is an accident and kids aren't wanted. It's too damn easy for men to fuck. They have no responsibility. It is always up to the woman. They are finally doing research on a male birth control pill. But look at all the time that's passed. Do they just figure men aren't responsible enough to use birth control? If men were the ones who got pregnant, wouldn't there be a lot more abortions? They wouldn't be able to play softball or drink their beer. What would they do? Abortion City."

"That really upsets you," Bonnie said.

"Yes, it does!" Julie said. "I know women who have used birth control, believing it's temporary. Then one day they want children and discover their birth control has forever ruined their chance of becoming pregnant. I spent time with a pregnant friend who had a wonderful husband. They wanted a family more than anything. She had to spend the whole pregnancy in bed. She went to the hospital, delivered a baby girl and four days later they buried her. Years earlier she used a method of birth control said to be safe and temporary, but because of it she could not carry a baby. Who felt the blame? She did because she used it."

Chapter 45

"WELL, I BELIEVE there is a man out there for me, my soul mate, and I will find him," I said.

"One of those guys from the bar the other night," Rebecca said laughing. We shared a private smile.

"You know, and what's so hard about being faithful? Why do we allow them to dog us? Why? Oh, because we love them. Then they keep dogging us. Why? Because we put up with it. You know, I know everybody makes mistakes, but those are not, 'Oops, I made a mistake,' mistakes. Those are mistakes that don't have to happen, that shouldn't happen," Veronica said.

"Fuckin' men!" Rebecca said.

"You can't blame all that on men. I blame the women just as much as I blame them," I said. "You know, women need to stick together. We need to respect each other enough so we don't have sex with married men."

"How can you say that? It's the guys who put themselves in those situations; they are the ones who can't say no," Rebecca said.

"I won't mention names, but I've seen women where you work go with married men, and they know they're married or involved in a relationship," Julie said.

"Yeah. No shit!" Rebecca got up and left the room.

"Nobody takes marriage seriously anymore, and my hope for a happy married life is fading," I said. " I was working front desk at a hotel years ago, and five women who worked there were sleeping with married men. And, yes, it'd be easy to blame the women for this, but I knew them and all they really wanted was to be loved. They were sad and lonely people. A man comes along and shows them attention and, Bam! they're in bed together. These women would fall in love with them and a week later the men are gone, business over. I remember answering the telephone, hearing the wife's voice. "Room three-o-eight, please."

"I'm sorry there's no answer, can I take a message?"

"Yes, will you tell him his wife called. Tell him I miss him and love him with all my heart."

"I sure will," I'd say, knowing he's sitting in the bar with Carol, who he's been screwing the past week."

"Poor women," Veronica said.

"Which women?" I asked.

"Both, the women at home being cheated on and the lonely women at the hotel."

"I don't see it that way. Those women at the hotel needed a hobby and to find love within themselves, from themselves. That's the problem," Julie said.

Chapter 46

"I DON'T KNOW, but I'll tell you what I did. I married myself," Veronica said.

"What?" Rebecca walked back in the room with a hand full of pretzels and a can of pop. "And, ah, how did all this happen?" Rebecca asked.

We all looked at each other and headed to the kitchen to munch. We sat around the table.

"Well, I'll tell you." She pulled her chair closer to the table. "One day I decided I would probably never get married, not because I did not want to, but because I just doubted I'd ever find that special man to share my life with. So instead of feeling sorry for myself and being lonely, I decided to treat myself like I would my marriage and husband. I married myself on June twenty-ninth, nineteen-ninety-five. I planned it; I even saved up for it. I went shopping for the ring, a beautiful dress, and I even made my honeymoon arrangements before the ceremony. It was an evening wedding. I had quite a few candles to light the room. I sat alone and made promises to myself, vows. As a matter of fact, I had them written up and framed. They're hanging in my living room by the front door. I see them everyday before leaving the house. It keeps me from feeling lonely. I know that sounds crazy, but it's true. Somebody very special made those promises to me. Now I do romantic things for myself. I treat myself to nice dinners out, or I order Chinese when I don't feel like cooking. I rent the movies I want to watch or go to the movie I want to see. I don't fight with myself over money or sex, and yes, I do date. I don't have to worry about cheating or depending. I treat myself better than I did before I was married. And if that special man does happen to come along, well I guess I'll just have two rings instead of one. I'll never divorce myself."

"So what'd ya do on your honeymoon?" Julie asked, reaching for her hand to see the ring.

"Well, I totally pampered myself. I stayed in a nice hotel and had a massage, facial, manicure, pedicure, mud bath; they cleansed and conditioned my hair. I had my brows shaped, my legs and bikini line waxed, and I had my colors done. I swam laps, went shopping during the day, had massages, and went out to fancy restaurants and theaters at night. I even had an escort the second night I was there, and no, I didn't pay him. I met him while I was out shopping. Anyway, that's what it was like. I treated myself like a queen. It was the best weekend of my life, and now I have my anniversaries to look forward to every year. I think everyone should do it, and not just women either. Most of us don't treat ourselves as good as we deserve. And there is always the pressure of getting married that sometimes causes us to make a mistake with our choice of a mate," Veronica said.

"I know what you mean. At age thirty, I'm starting to feel the pressure, not only from my parents, but from myself," Jody said.

"So what were your vows to yourself anyway?" Bonnie asked.

"Well, let's see, I have them pretty much memorized, but I do carry them with me in my wallet. They go like this: I will love you forever. I will treat you with respect. I will be responsible with choices. I will stay focused on goals. I will work hard to make a good living. I will not hurt you or let anyone else hurt you. I will be romantic with you. I will learn to love what I cannot change, and that doesn't include men. How many is that? "

"Eight."

"Well, they run on those lines. Oh, and I always pamper myself when I have my period, especially the first day. I usually take that day off and lie around, watch movies, take catnaps, and catch up on some reading. To me it's positive, it should be celebrated," Veronica said.

"I think that is so cool. I've never heard anything like that," I said. "Making promises to yourselves."

"Come on, you have to admit, it's kind of corny," Rebecca said.

"Well, the way I see it, we have to find crazy ways to make ourselves happy sometimes, especially when we're lonely. Then after you do it, and it helps, it doesn't seem so crazy. What's crazy is not doing good things for yourself, things to make you happy. Life is too short," Veronica added.

"You know what I did once? Oh, I don't know if I can tell," Bonnie said.

"Come on, what did you do?" Julie asked.

"Oh, OK, I'll tell you, but don't laugh."

"How can we laugh after what we just heard. It can't be any stranger," Rebecca said.

"Well, I was depressed. I had a new job in a new city and was alone. I had no boyfriend and hardly any friends. To make you all understand, my phone never rang. I was walking by a flower shop one evening on my way home from work and decided to step inside. I'll never forget the fragrance of that shop. I walked around for a while checking things out, wishing I had a man to send me flowers.

"Before I knew it, I was filling out a card. With disguised handwriting, I wrote something like, 'I think you're a very beautiful woman with a kind heart. Thinking of you often…' I sealed it in the envelope and handed it to the woman working. I told her I wanted to send flowers to my sister and they could pick them out. I told her the colors I wanted them to use and the amount of money I wanted to spend. I used cash when paying so they wouldn't see the name on the check, and used my middle name for the statement in case of a question or problem. I couldn't believe I did it, but it was great. It was exciting to get flowers delivered to me at work. Plus I got a little attention at the office from my coworkers. Then a week later I had them delivered to my home. It was going to be a long weekend, so, same kind of note, spent a little less money, and chose a different color, but it sure did lift my spirits. I know it was a lie, but…"

"I think it's great," I said.

"All right, here's one I've done. I didn't like my past, so I did some meditation and changed it," Bonnie said and put her fingertips in her mouth to bite her nails.

"What do you mean?" Rebecca asked.

I knew what Bonnie was about to say, and it was clear she was reluctant to tell.

"Well, I was…well, my dad sexually assaulted me for three and a half years of my life. It started when I was about twelve. A drunk driver killed my mother in a car accident when I was eleven years old. Not long after, my father started drinking, involving himself in pornography, and I believe he was doing some drugs too. He couldn't handle the fact his wife, my mother, was no longer around. It didn't take long before his whole world crumbled, and I was beneath it when it fell.

"I was a little girl running a high fever. I was in my bed crying for my mommy. My father was in the living room sitting in his chair, in the dark, drinking his whiskey from the bottle. He could hear me crying and didn't know what to do to comfort me. He had finished the last of his bottle and decided to check on me.

"He staggered down the hall to my room and stood in my doorway watching me. My fever turned to a chill, and I started shivering. I cried for my mom to hold me. He set his empty bottle down where he stood and came into my room. He crawled in bed next to me to keep me warm. I held onto him tight for warmth. His pelvis began to move, pressing against me. His breathing became shaky and he started touching me."

With a tear running down her cheek, Bonnie gently smiled and said, "I'll stop there. Anyway, I felt terrible guilt my whole life, not only because my mom died on her way to pick me up from a friend's house, but that night, I felt like it was my fault my dad did that to me. Why would I cry for my mother when I knew she was dead and my dad couldn't do anything to bring her back to us? My dad missed her too. So how could I do that to him? Guilt is the worst!"

"I'm so sorry," Julie said.

"No, now I am not telling you this to get pity," she said wiping her eyes. "I'm just letting you know how I fixed it, and that's the fun part. After all the truths came to the surface and I was taken away, I felt dirty and trapped inside this body, so I'd read a book and be taken away. I always wanted to leave my body, so I started reading up on meditation and soul travel. That is where I found my answers. I decided my past and my future are only illusions. I've learned the only thing important is the present."

Leaning forward she touched Julie and herself and the table and Sara saying, "See I can touch it, I can feel it, it's real. I can't feel yesterday or tomorrow; they can't be touched, but I can feel today, the here and now. So I changed my past in my mind, body, and spirit. My past was ruining my present and future. My guilt and shame together were mapping out my life. I put an end to that. Through my meditation, I have traveled in time to relive and change the bad memories in my past. I have relived this life over and over again, and it's what I live by."

She paused. "My parents and I were in a terrible car accident when I was about eleven. Both my parents died, and I was in a coma for about three years. When I came out of it I was put in intense therapy, where I started reading books to ease my mind. One of the most disturbing books I've ever read was about a little girl who was being assaulted by her father. And that is why I do the work I do, to save money and go to school so I can help little boys and little girls when something in their life goes wrong. So I can help put away the people who do these things to innocent children."

"That's incredible, I can't believe we don't know each other better," Sara said drying her eyes.

Sara had been sitting quietly looking like an outcast. I had hoped she would join the group, and she did.

"Everybody, we need to make a promise to each other. Everything you hear during this party has to stay here. This stuff can't be talked about after the party is over. It's too personal and too serious. Is it a deal?" Julie asked.

Everybody agreed.

Then Sara asked, "How do you do it, the soul traveling?"

"Well, I could help you, or I could loan you some books. Sometimes it is a real personal thing and it's easier to be alone. Just let me know, OK? I'll help you if you have questions," Bonnie said.

"I'm really interested."

"I'm glad. It's helped me. I also use it to help with my goals. I make my future what I want, just like I did my past. I meditate with my past and future, so I can keep the present in perspective, in focus," Bonnie added.

"That's all fine and dandy, Bonnie, but you're a stripper! What goals? What future?"

"I won't be there much longer. Isn't that what this party is about anyway? Besides I think the trouble in our lives is what has brought us all together. We all want more. Angie was the initiator."

Rebecca rolled her eyes. "OK, I have one. I like to go out, get drunk, wild, and laid," Rebecca said.

"That's it, you go sit in the corner. It's time out for you," Julie said and everybody laughed. "What is your story anyway?"

"Maybe some other time," Rebecca said.

"Well maybe you should think about marrying yourself, sending yourself flowers for a month, and doing some soul travel and meditation," Jody joked.

Surprisingly, even Rebecca laughed at that, but even harder when Sara informed us she was going to try it.

"Which one?" I asked.

She answered seriously, "All of them."

When the laughing stopped I said, "I did something to change my life, kind of. I took ten years off my life. I felt like at twenty-six years old I really hadn't achieved much, so I decided if I were sixteen, I would feel differently about what I had done in my lifetime. I felt young and excited about life, I made up reasons why I wasn't in school and had a lot of fun with the fantasy for about a month. Now anytime I need a lift I do that. It adds a little spark to my life. After doing it, it made me think differently about age, and I feel like sometimes in some people that number just means how tired you are of living."

Chapter 47

"HAVE ANY OF you had those problems with controlling men?" Veronica asked.

"Who hasn't!" Julie began. "That type of man never deserves a second chance. You have to get him out of your life as soon as you figure it out. No matter how much you care about him."

"It's hard to break up, no matter what the situation. One time I went through a hard break up. I felt sad and lonely, all the time questioning, wondering if I should go back to him. So I made a list of things to do that made me feel good. Like when I got lonely for him, I'd go rent movies and munch on popcorn or go for a walk. But my favorite thing to do was go to the Humane Society and play with all the cats and dogs. The last time I was there I came home with a friend, a black kitten I named Shadow. Now he's there for me in hard times. He's my best friend," Veronica said.

"Speaking of lists, I make one out of all the mean things he's ever done to me, all the times he hurt me and whenever I feel weak and lonely for him I take out my list. I change my mind about missing him," I said. "It goes from loneliness to pride for getting him out of my life. If I lose myself in a relationship, I lose everything."

"A good friend of mine got herself mixed up in a relationship with a very controlling man," said Julie. "She'd call me, tell me about how she'd have a hard time saying what she wanted and that she was getting really confused about her feelings. She wasn't ready to leave the relationship yet, but she felt she needed a little support.

"So I told her to leave the room anytime things didn't feel quite right so she could be alone and make decisions with clear thoughts. She said she'd go to the bathroom every time she felt controlled, so she wouldn't be talked into something she really didn't want. Well, about three days later she called me to tell me she broke up with him. Instead of allowing people to wonder if she had a bladder problem, she went to the bathroom in her mind. She'd block out people around her and pretend she was in a room alone, making her own choices, her own decisions. She said she stuck to those and realized this was not the guy for her," Julie said.

"You know, I've spent so much of my time with losers, people I knew deep down wouldn't amount to a good partner. Then along with that, of course, came me trying to change them," Jody said. "I think it was loneliness and just wanting someone around. Each time a bad relationship ended I felt bad, like a failure, when I knew we never should've been together in the first place."

"Sounds familiar," I said. "I think I chose unhealthy men so I would never be in a long-term relationship. I was afraid, and I thought it kept me safe. But it didn't, of course. And the breakups still hurt."

Julie stood, stretched and said, "On the other side of it, sometimes you have so many failed relationships in the past your heart can't take another one. So you stay and fight for it even though you know you're not happy."

"I know men aren't objects, even though they like to consider *us* to be. But I feel like I go to the car lot wanting a pickup truck and somehow I end up going home with a VW Bug. I kind of like the Bug, but I know I really needed the pickup. So I put it in my garage, cut off the back, and get big tires and a roll bar. But it's still just a Bug. That's what I do with men. Maybe it's because I've never met a pickup. Is it better to settle for a Bug or completely be without?" Jody asked.

"Be without. It won't work, because all you're doing is screwing him up. What if there are women out there who really want a Bug? They could be happy together. Plus, look at all the work you're doing for nothing. He'll never be a pickup truck and one day you'll realize that, after you've put in a lot of time, money, and hard work. Then you'll be mad at him, and you'll resent him, but it wasn't his fault, because you *were* the Mustang that he wanted. Besides, why do *we* think he'll be happier as a truck?" Julie asked.

"OK, enough about cars. Who wants to get into my car with me and go to Taco Bell before they close?" Bonnie asked.

Sara wanted to go.

We all placed our order and put in a few bucks.

Chapter 48

VERONICA YELLED IN from the living room, "Can I turn up your stereo, Julie?

She entered the kitchen and said, "I love this song. I love music."

We all agreed it was a great song.

"You know what I mean, it always makes you feel better or worse. And that's just it, it brings out your emotions so you can deal with them instead of burying them and waiting for the explosion to deal with them. To change your mood is as easy as switching the station or CD."

"And besides all that, if you get the right kind of music it makes you want to dance, and that's great exercise and fun. And I could take that a step farther and say just how wonderful exercise and working out with weights can be," Jody said. "Not only for your body, but for your self-esteem as well. You can be going through boyfriend problems, money problems, anything. Go to the gym, lift some weights and you'll feel so good you won't want a man. You'll want something harder... Iron!"

"Ha, ha." Julie threw in a little sarcasm.

"Do you lift weights so guys won't be attracted to you?" Rebecca asked.

In a stupid sounding sarcastic voice Julie said, "Yeah, are you a lesbian?"

We all started laughing.

"Well, I've thought about it, haven't you?" Veronica asked.

Julie started laughing, "Either you are, or you're not. You can't just decide to be a lesbian."

"You can't?" I asked with a giggle.

"Well, I have no curiosity about it. I had a bad experience once with a girlfriend of mine," Julie said.

"What happened?" Jody asked.

"Well, my friend and I were getting ready to go out dancing. I was in my early twenties. Both of us were excited and drinking while fussing over our clothes, make up, and hair. We were fighting over who would get the best looking guy and who'd get lucky, common talk for my friends and me. It wasn't really what we were looking for, but it always seemed to keep the excitement and competition alive for fun.

"Drinking, dancing, and fun, we were having a blast. My friend had met a man early on and spent most of the time with him kissing, drinking, and making plans for the rest of the night. I, on the other hand, was spreading my attention around like every other night. I was flirting, boosting egos, and shocking the men I met. Both she and I were drinking heavily.

"It was bar close and time to go back to the hotel where we were staying for the night. I had a great night and was excited to get to my bed and dream about the one beautiful fun man that I had met that night. My friend had a different kind of night planned. We were supposed to take a cab home, but this guy my friend picked up, or who picked her up, however you want to look at it, wanted to take us home. So I got in the back seat. She got in and sat next to him, and he drove us to the hotel.

I crawled right into bed with my clothes on. I made a phone call while I watched my friend go back and forth from the bathroom to the bed area. She was getting ready for her soon-to-be-lover, who was in the other bed, also watching her and trying to talk to me. I hung up the phone and rolled over. Shortly after I heard her get into bed and the light went out. I listened for a while, to the kissing, giggling, and whispering, and I fell asleep.

I woke up shortly after with both of them in my bed, next to me. I was drunk and disgusted. I couldn't believe what was happening. My friend was saying, "Julie wouldn't like this; let's go back to the other bed."

He said, "No, she'll like it, it's OK."

"I felt his hand reach over to me, and he tried to rub between my legs. Every time I tried to push him away he would grab my hand and place it on my friend. As this was going on I realized my friend was rubbing my breast. I frantically pushed them both away from me. She moved over to the other bed and he kept attempting to be with me. I pushed him again and noticed my friend had turned her back on this situation and me. I could not believe this, and I was scared to death. She brought him here, and now I was the one who had to deal with this shit, and without her help.

"He was sitting on the bed naked with an erection. It was too dark to make out his facial expression, but I was terrified. He was twice my size, maybe even three times. It looked to me like he was sitting there debating what to do next. He wasn't saying anything, just staring like he could snap at any moment. I cocked my foot back and gave a hard push to his ass. If he hadn't stood, he would've fallen onto the floor. I didn't know what to do. In an assertive tone I said, "Get the fuck out of here!" I tried to make it sound as if he didn't have a choice.

"He stood there for what seemed like half an hour, then bent over and started picking up his clothes. I sat leaning against the headboard with my arms crossed in front of my chest watching him. He left, and I got up and locked the door behind him.

"I went to lie back down, and kept thinking about how we were supposed to be safe—staying in a hotel, taking a cab to and from the bar, and having harmless fun. Knowing what you plan on doing and what you end up doing on alcohol are two different things. With that thought I fell asleep.

"The next morning my friend was no longer my friend. I was so uncomfortable around her. Neither of us talked about it. We just walked around the room collecting our things, making small talk, and avoiding each other as much as possible. I didn't want to blame her, but I did. I was angry at her for letting it happen. She was the one who brought him home. He was her responsibility and she didn't take care of the problem. The only thing she said about it was, 'What happened last night? I fell asleep.'

"I kicked him out," I said. And that was it. Our friendship was over.

"I don't regret ending the relationship, but I do regret that night. I've had to forgive both of them. The hardest was forgiving myself, and I've done that too. That night made an important impact on my life. The realization started taking place the second I locked the door of the hotel room. I was making poor choices in my life, for myself.

"As a little girl, all the way through to being a young woman, I never once dreamed of hanging out in bars, drinking heavily, picking up strange men, and having lousy friends. I had to step back, take a look, and make changes in my life. I changed my regret to a blessing, and I'm thankful I woke up and faced the reality of where my life was headed."

"That's a very positive way of looking at it, like a gift. That takes a lot of strength," Veronica said.

"Thanks."

"Well, the way I see it is I have never met a man who could really understand my feelings, especially about women's issues. I know another woman would understand."

"Yeah, well, I've met a lot of women who view things just like men," I said. "My sister's one of them. I wanted to smack her upside the head one day. We went to my mother's house to pick something up and two women were working on the phone wires. She said, 'I don't know why they sent a woman to do a man's job.' She sounded like she was eighty years old or a man, I couldn't believe it."

"That's only because men've shaped women like your sister, like clay. They've turned these women into what they want them to be and how they want them to think," Julie said.

"Anyway, Rebecca, I'm not a lesbian." Jody said. "You sound like Angie's sister. Just because I have muscle, I must like women or want to be a man."

"Yeah, some people think if a woman doesn't have a boyfriend or if she doesn't wear makeup, well, then she must be gay," Veronica said.

"Or if she doesn't like to wear dresses, or she doesn't like to go shopping. Gay," Jody added.

"Oh, I remember one time, I was being interviewed for a job by a man. I got the job, and about six months later I started spending time with one of his friends who informed me everybody there thought I was a lesbian. Why? Because in the interview I told him I was a writer. He asked me what I wrote about and I said, 'women's issues.' And just because of that he assumed I was gay. He told everyone I was into women!" I said.

"I think most guys think all women are lesbians to some extent," Veronica said.

"Men can be so stupid," Jody said. "But so can women."

"I'm not gay either, but I'll tell you something about my younger years. My friends and I were going through puberty so we'd get together and do things with our bodies," I said.

"Like what kind of things?"

"We would take turns touching and looking at each others private parts while the others watched. We'd do things like Joni would lie on her back with her legs up over her head so we could look at her anus. God, we used to laugh because she would squeeze then push. There wasn't a lot of touching; we just wanted to know how our bodies were changing. We were experimenting. I think most normal kids do, but don't admit it," I said.

"Yeah, I wouldn't admit it," Rebecca said.

Everybody laughed.

"And then there is that masturbation thing. Who didn't feel guilty for masturbating?" Jody asked. "I didn't know anything until a friend showed me and told me about it. Her mom had a vibrator and her dad had the Playboy Channel. He had that silver tube filter thing, but my friend knew where he kept it and we used to watch it. I didn't know anything until she and her sister taught me. Maybe we were all too young to know about that stuff, too young to see it."

"That's a good point. You're right, Jod," Julie said. "Young people just shouldn't be exposed to it. Adults either, for that matter."

Chapter 49

WE FINISHED EATING our Taco Bell and went back into the living room.

"Speaking of God…" Veronica, said. "What do you think about the Bible?"

"Hmmm, that's a tough one. I really don't believe much in the Bible," Julie said.

"I don't either. Why don't you believe in it?" Veronica asked.

"I don't know. My spirituality comes from something greater than a bunch of words put together by God only knows who… no pun intended. You know, I used to belong to a church where women couldn't usher, help with collection or communion. And a woman couldn't do any speaking. My God didn't give me every capability as man just so 'he' could tell me I can't do certain things man can," Julie said. "Besides, the only known women in the Bible are either prostitutes or virgins. Which leads me to believe it's just a sick man's fun book."

"I tried to read it," I said. "But every time I picked up the Bible, I'd get through Genesis and be ill. The first twenty pages I learned giving birth is punishment. Because of the apple thing, men can rule over us. Men and sons are the important ones. And men were sodomizing other males so a father offered his two virgin daughters instead, and it said something like, because that's the way it should be. And two daughters got their dad drunk so they could have sex with him and have a baby. That's all I could take, and I don't pick it up any more. After I read this, I decided to get some help from a pastor. So I called a church. I asked him questions over the phone and tried not to laugh at his answers. I asked him if women can do the offering, greeting and help with the communion at his church. He said they did have some women who enjoy helping during service. Then I asked him if they had women ministers there. He said women had a complete ministry in the congregation without preaching the word. Women weren't allowed to preach the word."

"No kidding?" Jody asked.

"Call around, you'll see," I said.

"I went to a Unity church for a while that I loved. They never referred to God as him or masculine, God was always, The Mother/Father God. I wish I could have moved my church with me when I moved. I've looked but have never found one like it, a close congregation and spiritual, not all about the Bible. It was about life and being a good person. I loved it," Julie said.

"Do you ever think about why we're here? Isn't it overwhelming? And why is it men made 'man' with 'w-o' in front of it for us, and a 'f-e', in front of male. In the other cultures, they are completely different words. So how was the Bible rewritten putting wo in front of man?" Veronica asked.

"Well, I don't know, but I'm going to kick back." Julie threw her legs over the arm of the oversized chair she was sitting in.

"Great idea," Veronica said and unbuttoned her pants.

We all giggled and got more comfortable ourselves.

"I hate it when people tell me I have to be a certain way in order to go to heaven. People try to judge me when they're on earth with me as an equal, not a superior. I was married and working at a restaurant. My husband was abusive, and sometimes I'd go to work wearing the evidence. One day a man came up to me and asked if he could talk to me in private. I said OK, afraid he would say something about the bruises. Well, he didn't mention them. He did mention that it didn't look like I was following my role as a woman. He gave me literature on religion and what my role is as a woman. He told me to read it and obey what it said and my life would not be so hard. I couldn't believe it." I said shaking my head.

"That's awful," Bonnie said and grabbed the throw pillow sitting next to her and set it on her lap then hugged it to her chest.

"Yeah, and what about priests molesting little boys," Julie demanded. "And all the adultery going on in churches."

"I went to a church where there was a family everybody looked up to. But at home, the kids were neglected. My aunt, who also went to this church, had to take one of their sons to the doctor because his parents wouldn't. He had a fungus growing on his feet causing them to peel and crack. They just kept telling him he needed to wash his feet better, like it was his fault," Jody said.

"It's so personal, I think, because we all have different experiences. But people say we should live for God. I say 'no' to that and always will. I don't live my life for God. I live my life for myself, because God is already inside me, so by living my life for me I'm living my life for God. We have the gift of life. It's sad when we don't use it," I said.

"Plus, it's fake to be good for God so you can go to heaven. What about being a good person just to be a good person, getting nothing in return?" Julie asked. "*We* are our God's eyes, our God's ears, and our God's hands and feet," she said. "Why pray for help when *you* can help? Pray to who, a power not on this earth? We are the power on this earth."

"And there is something else I question. Think about the order of creation. God made the water, then land, next the plants, then the animals, on to man, and last the woman. So if you look at the order, who is superior?" I asked. "God started at the bottom and worked up to the top. Woman."

"And what if we are the superior ones and always have been, but because men were stronger than us, came to power over us, turning all the good in us into bad and even making us think it's bad. The only time we're good is when we're serving them or raising their babies. Ya know these aren't the caveman days anymore. And while some men are physically stronger, most women are emotionally stronger. In time we'll go farther."

"I'll be right back," I said. I stood to go to the kitchen, where I left my diet Coke.

Leaving the room I heard, "Well, man was made from the dust of the earth to rule over the earth. Woman was made from the rib of man to rule over men. It makes perfect sense to me."

I smiled to myself and entered the kitchen. Sara was sitting there alone.

Chapter 50

"SARA, WHY AREN'T you in with the rest of us?" I asked.

"Oh, I was just thinking, I wanted a little time alone," she said. "You know, I've never had people around like you and Julie. You're all so strong, and it makes me want to be strong."

I could tell she was about to break down, so I grabbed her hand and we walked into Julie's bedroom, turned the light on, and closed the door. I turned toward her, and she started to cry. She collapsed on the bed. "The other girls don't like me because of my breasts," she said.

"How do you know? Have you ever given them a chance to get to know you?"

"No, I can't. It hurts too bad."

"What do you mean?"

"I can't because they always hurt me. I can't let them close because I'm afraid."

I watched her cry. I couldn't believe the difference between this woman now and the woman I interviewed. Her strong exterior was gone, and I couldn't understand why she let it go with me. She lay back on the bed crying, her hands covering her face as if to hide it from me. I sat down next to her and put my hand on her shoulder. "Sara, are you OK?"

After a long pause, "No, Angie, I'm not."

"What's wrong?" I asked. "Why are you hurting like this?"

"You know why, can't you see it?" she asked.

"No, I don't know what you mean."

She sat back up, "Look at my life. Look at what it's become. Look at what I've become."

"Sara. You can change it. You have that power, and you know what? You're the only one who has that power," I said. "It's never so bad you can't turn things around."

"You don't know… It's bad, really bad."

"Do you want to talk about it?"

"No, you'll hate me."

"Sara, we all make mistakes. We get through 'em. If I can help, I want to."

She was crying hard. She looked at me as she was trying to read me, trying to see past what I was saying.

"I'm not a judge. I can't judge you. I'm far from perfect. Believe me, you have not made any worse mistakes than I have."

She looked surprised but disbelieving.

"If you're not ready to talk that's fine, but I'm here if you need to. OK?"

I leaned over and gave her a hug. She gently said in my ear, "Angie, I've done trains." She started crying again, but this time it was more of a silent cry with out-of-control tears. I broke my hold on her and faced her.

"Sara, do you mean… How did it happen?"

"Well, the first time, I was drinking a lot and this one guy was showing me a lot of attention. We were at a party. He asked if I wanted to go into one of the rooms and make love. I was feeling pretty high and thought he seemed nice, so I agreed. After we were finished, he told me he had a friend who liked me and asked if he could go get him. I really didn't understand what he meant. I thought he was saying he wanted this guy to see I was with him and I was off limits, so to speak.

"Well, his friend came in, and I was kind of out of it from being tired and high from the alcohol. He started touching me, and before I knew it I was making out with him and it happened. The thought of me being with two guys in one night excited me at the time so when the third came in I went for it, and the fourth. The next morning when I woke up, I was sick. I vomited all morning. I felt so dirty and used. It hurt. I never wanted to be like that. I know this sounds dumb, but I really liked that first guy and I thought he liked me. I never saw him again.

"The second time, also at a party. One of the guys who had me before was there and told most of the guys about it. I had been drinking again, so when he came up to me and started talking nice to me, telling me I was beautiful and he wanted to kiss me, I was flattered. And it went from there. The last time, I started crying. I was just with one guy, the first guy, and I knew it was going to happen. I started crying while he was having sex with me. I told him to get off me; I grabbed my clothes and got dressed. I reached over to the phone on the nightstand and called a cab. I left the party, and I haven't been to another one, until this one. That was about two months ago."

"I'm really proud of you to put a stop to that type of treatment. You should be proud, too."

"Men think the only thing I'm good for is sex. They think my body was made for their enjoyment, like I'm a ride in an amusement park, nothing more. And what's really sad is most of the time I feel they're right," Sara said.

"Sara, you're worth so much more than that!"

She broke a long silence. "I did have a boyfriend once, who I lived with. I used to do all kinds of things for him, which had nothing to do with sex. I kept the house clean, made nice dinners, sometimes with candles for romance. I'd buy him little gifts and leave notes for him to let him know I loved him, and he did it all in return for me. He was so good to me. I even built him a shelf in our closet one time and surprised him with it. I made him a cake from scratch, for his birthday. It took me two hours. He couldn't believe I did it. It was his favorite cake, red velvet cake. He treated me so good. I loved doing things for him."

She started crying. "I wish he was still in my life."

"What happened to him?"

"Well… he was always active in sports, especially hockey. So he played every Wednesday evening with a group of guys. We got engaged on a Saturday night. That next Wednesday he played hockey. He had an accident while he was there and came home early. I guess he hit his head on the ice pretty hard. I asked him if he wanted to go in to the hospital; he said he'd rather wait a little while to see if he felt better. I didn't know how bad it was. About an hour later, I heard him making noises in our bedroom. I hollered to him, but he didn't answer so I ran in... He was laying there in convulsions. I was so scared I must have stood there for a minute, frozen. Finally, I called 911. By the time we got to the hospital, he had gone into a coma. He died shortly after."

She was calm while telling me.

"The strange thing is after he asked me to marry him, we made love, then lay in bed talking into the morning. We talked about everything. One thing he did say to me that night was if anything ever happened to him he wanted me to move on with my life and remarry if another 'right one' came along.

"After about a year and a few months of loneliness I decided to start dating. I was so angry he had left me, and I wanted him back so badly. Well, I guess I tried to find him in these men, but the only thing they wanted from me was to try me out, because of my breasts. I always ended up feeling so dirty and used. And the whole time I was just trying to find someone to love me, the way he did. Now here I am in this mess. I cry myself to sleep thinking about how he's in heaven watching me, and how disappointed he must feel."

"No, Sara, he's looking down and he's angry with them, because he knows what a beautiful person you are. He knows those guys are making terrible mistakes not seeing that. He is proud of you right now. He knows you're hurting. I will support you in changes you want to make. I will help you any way I can. A friend always used to say to me, you help you, and I'll help you, too. You know, I knew you were strong the first time I saw you. Oh! You pissed me off!" I shook my head and grinned. "But I liked you... maybe we all just need each other right now."

"Thanks, Angie."

"Sara, you are very special, don't let anyone take that away from you." I got up and got the box of Kleenex from the other side of the bed. We both wiped away our tears and blew our noses. I was blowing my nose when a loud horn like sound squealed out. We both started laughing. "Should we join the crowd?"

"Yes, thanks for everything," she said as we hugged.

"You're welcome. Let's go see what they're griping about now."

Chapter 51

EVERYBODY WAS BACK in the kitchen. A bag of Hershey's Miniatures was acting as a centerpiece. "What's going on in here?" I said holding hands with Sara.

"We wanted something sweet," Julie said.

"We're talking about things that keep us down in this world we live in," Rebecca said.

"Besides strip bars?" I asked, and Sara and I sat down next to each other at the table.

Julie laughed, "That's right."

Jody walked back into the kitchen from the bathroom. She must have heard Rebecca, and said, "I'll start. OK, when you see men, usually coaches, cops, or other men in a superior position over other men or boys. They call them girls, ladies, women. It is such an insult toward women, like we're so weak. 'Come on ladies' or 'You're nothing but a bunch of girls.' It's not a put down to the guys, it's a put down to us women."

"That's a good one," Rebecca said.

"One day while I was writing, I was looking through the dictionary for a word when I saw 'slut' on the top of page 857. I could not believe that slang word was in there. So of course, I started looking up other derogatory words toward women. It had 'bitch,' 'whore,' 'tit,' and 'slut,' all with definitions against women. I then tried to find some derogatory words toward men and only found 'bastard,' which wasn't associated with male or female. And I realized there really aren't any bad words toward men. Of course the dictionary was edited by all men: general editor, man; associate general editor, man; senior editor, man; associate editors, man, man, man; managing editor, man. Oh, and of course the term 'gentle sex' was women in general. Plus, 'son of a bitch,' doesn't even rip on the man, it's the man's mother, the woman," I said.

"That good old Mr. and Mrs. has always bugged me. It might as well be Mr. with an apostrophe s. When you get married you become his, marked with his name and all," Veronica said, "Even though that's changing."

"Yes, thank God. Some men still have a hard time with women not wanting to take their last name," Jody said. "At least some of the guys I've dealt with have. They think if they can change your name they feel they can take away your identity."

"How about when male police officers want you to step out of your car?" Bonnie said.

"Or has this ever happened to you? A cop pulled me over for drinking when I was young and wild, driving a bit fast. He told me he could take me in, but decided to let me go with a warning. Then he started harassing me all the time. Anytime he saw me, he would stop me to see how I was doing. He would stop by my work and tell me about his personal life and marital problems. I moved shortly afterwards, but I think he thought he had something over me and wanted to use that to get me into bed or something," Veronica said.

"Mud flaps," Julie said. "I hate those mud flaps on semis. They should be banned. That sends a terrible message out to all people. Most people see them and think nothing of it, but think of the little girls and little boys who see that stuff every day. No matter what people say, it does make an impact on people's lives. What would you tell your little girl if she asked you about them, or even your little boy? What would you say? 'Why is that picture of a woman on those mud flaps like that, Mom?'"

"How about the times you lock your keys in the car. Who usually comes to help…a man. He walks up like Mr. Stud himself coming to rescue the damsel in distress. One man walked right up to my car and started to try to get in. I told him, back the fuck up! Did I ask for your help? If a man's kind about it and doesn't offend me, then maybe I'll listen to what he has to say. But usually I just thank him for the offer and send him on his way. I can get into my car myself!" Jody exclaimed.

"Yeah, only because you lock your keys in all the time," Rebecca said jokingly.

"So what. I can help any of you with that if you ever have that problem," Jody teased.

"I remember on the news, a woman who was a madam was in trouble. She claimed she was only helping women. That made me sick. It's like selling your own kind as slaves and then claiming to help them," Veronica said.

"I may be stepping out on a limb here, because some of you may like it: pornographic movies and magazines for men, though some women watch them, too. Do women not realize that some woman is making the film? Would they want to make a porno or be in a pornographic magazine air brushed and spread eagle for the world to see? Probably not, but *some* woman is," I said. "Plus pornography is an addiction and can lead to so many other problems. It promotes sexual violence against women. Women and children are victimized repeatedly through pornography, yet the First Amendment protects anyone who wants to sell, produce, and be involved in pornography. And that silences all women. What about our rights? What about the rights of the innocent children who are abducted to help produce child pornography, and then are killed, or sold to the streets because they've outgrown child porn? What about their rights? Who protects them?"

"Besides, women couldn't even vote when the First Amendment was made. We were property. We were slightly above cattle. Times are changing, and women need to stand up and fight for those changes," Julie protested as she stood and left the room.

"Wow!" Jody said. "I guess I never really thought about it. She's right."

"I was reading a non-pornographic magazine one day, and there was a quote from a male actor. It said something about how it's not man's fault, it's their hormones that keep them from being morally right, and God made it that way so they can't be blamed," Veronica said. "So basically he's admitting that he doesn't have a brain."

We all laughed.

"That's disgusting! What a pig," Rebecca said. "But that magazine thing is another thing that bugs me. Almost all women's magazines are telling women we're not good enough the way we are. We need to lose ten pounds fast. We need to know how to make our man happy in bed. We need to know how to flatten our stomachs and reduce our hips. They give us makeup tricks—how to make our lips look fuller, our nose smaller. The list goes on and on, on ways we need to improve ourselves as women. Men's magazines just tell them who's doing good in sports. Oh, and they always throw in that swimsuit issue for them as an added bonus."

"I was watching a children's movie the other day with my nieces, and I was shocked by the messages in that film," I said. "It was an animated movie. There was a woman with large breasts, and it had men staring at her chest, then one man was hit over the head by, I guess, his wife, like it was cute. Another part showed a man who wanted to be rich. He started singing a song about how if he were rich all the women would love him. It was awful for kids to see, I thought. Like that's all women want from men is money. One other time I was watching Saturday morning cartoons, and Bugs Bunny was fighting a witch. At the end of the cartoon the witch turned into a sexy female bunny, so Bugs approached her and they started walking away arm in arm. Then Bugs turned to the camera and said, "Yeah, I know, but aren't they all witches on the inside anyway?""

"You're lying!" Julie said walking back into the room.

"No, I'm not!"

"See what I mean?" Julie questioned and she looked at everybody. "What does that tell our sons and daughters? What does it say to us? And we accept this?"

Chapter 52

I WENT TO the bathroom not only to use the toilet, but to get a break. I was exhausted. I expected an empowering night. I took my time washing my hands with the strawberry-scented soap.

When I came back, I fell into the new topic of conversation, money.

"Well, why are you a stripper?" Julie asked.

"For the money," Rebecca and Bonnie said at the same time.

Julie jumped right in, "So you're prostitutes!

They jumped back at her, "No, we're not!"

"You're selling your body for money. That's prostitution," Julie shot back. "I mean, it certainly can't be because it's fun. You all have dark circles under your eyes," she added. "You can't be that happy working there and having all that money."

"It can be really hard on the spirit," Veronica said. "It's tough to go day after day dealing with the kind of men we deal with, trying to look beautiful and sexy."

"As if you ever try," Rebecca teased.

Looking as if she were caught, Veronica smiled and said, "Well, you have a point."

"Something in society put you there. As little girls, you don't dream of one day being a stripper. Little girls are taught things in our society, or, maybe a better way of putting it, little girls are victimized in our society," Julie said. "There is no question that women who want to strip have gone through something to lower their self worth, period."

"That is so true. At age eleven, a friend of the family molested me. I still didn't know what sex was, but I think I had an idea. I found myself fantasizing about being a prostitute, at age eleven."

"That's really sad," Sara said. "At that age, you're not even thinking about making a living."

"Yes, it is sad, and it's taken me years to understand it," I said.

"What's the worst thing you've ever done for money?" Jody asked, for anyone to answer.

"Besides being a prostitute," Julie added.

"I took money I found in a restaurant. I found a checkbook that had about a hundred dollars cash inside. I was so poor at the time, I took it. If it was a test, I failed. But if it was a gift, I'm thankful. It came at a time when I really needed it. I kept one check deposit slip for her name and address, and now that I'm doing better financially, I'm going to pay her back with an added bonus," I said.

"Wow, how long ago did you take it?" Sara asked.

"About two years ago."

"Why did you need it?"

"I was homeless and lived in my car."

"Why?"

"I don't know. Sometimes we just get stuck."

"What was it like?" Veronica asked.

"It was tough." I hesitated. I didn't want to get into it.

Julie must have sensed it and interrupted with, "I never did like numbers, not age, time, and especially not the numbers on dollar bills."

"Yeah, but when you have money you can do anything, and go anywhere," Rebecca said.

"No, you can't love somebody or be loved by somebody just because you have money. I think you can easily miss out on all the really important things in life, the little things that mean the most," Sara said.

"I'd rather go for a walk in the rain than worry about ruining my five hundred dollar dress in it. Or making sure the limo driver gets close enough to the door so that you don't get wet and mess up your hair," Julie added.

"That's the sweet romantic stuff whether you're with a man or alone, a closeness you can't get in a fancy restaurant or opening night at the opera,"

Veronica said. "Or even driving in a fancy car or living in a great apartment. Money can't buy the heart stuff."

"You know that is so true. Although I had hard times while living in my car, they were some of the best times of my life. I'll never forget waking up to rain softly pattering against my windows in the middle of the night, or waking up to my car being covered with snow."

"You were homeless in the winter time?" Sara asked.

"Yes."

"I could never do that," Jody said.

"You could if you had to; it's called survival. And that's when you realize just how strong you really are."

Chapter 53

I DECIDED IT would be a good time for me to lie down for awhile. It had been a long day and night; my brain was tired of thinking, and I was exhausted. I walked into Julie's room and closed the door behind me. I grabbed her throw blanket off the foot of the bed and covered myself as I lay down. Right away, I felt my body relaxing as I fell into a deep sleep.

I dreamed of a childhood memory. At age thirteen or maybe fourteen, I was going through puberty and at night, in my bedroom while sleeping, I would touch myself, unaware of it until this night.

My door was open, which was common. Either I was scared when I went to bed or my mother forgot to close it after checking on me before going to bed herself. I was asleep and my mom's boyfriend, who always seemed to get out of bed in the middle of the night to eat, walked by my room. I woke just enough to realize he had entered my room and was sitting next to me on my bed.

"What are you doing, Ang?" he asked.

I ignored him and continued lying there with my eyes closed and heart beating rapidly.

Again, "Ang, what are you doing?"

I slightly opened my eyes and realized he was naked. My heart was pounding in fear. I rolled over onto my side with my back facing him. He started laughing an evil laugh. I was scared.

What was this man doing in my room, late at night, on my bed, naked? Did he think I was horny or wanted him because I was touching myself in my sleep? Did he think it was funny? Did he laugh at me to make me feel dirty? Didn't he realize that he was scaring me? Did he care?

I was a young woman going through puberty, that's it!

I woke feeling sad and lonely, remembering the dream, and remembering that night. It led me to thoughts of my life and my own sexuality. A person's sexuality can be so misunderstood. And to a young woman, so confusing. I thought of other things that were just as confusing to me. Like waiting to lose your virginity in marriage because a good friend of your mother's, who you looked up to, did. And you thought their marriage was good and strong and healthy because of it.

Then after saving yourself for that special man, discovering that he would rather hit you than love you. And finding out your mom's friend's husband, the one who took her virginity on their wedding night, molested your sister for about a year.

Or being married for six months and being really scared and insecure about it because things are not going the way you had hoped. So you go away with your mom for a weekend on one of her business trips, undressing in the bathroom so she doesn't see the bruises your husband had given you before you left. Then sitting at a restaurant with her, wanting her to help you understand, even though you can't tell her what's happening. Hoping she will say something to help you. But the only thing she cares to share with you is that while she was pregnant with you, your father had an affair with your sister's babysitter.

Or leaving your abusive husband with thoughts of suicide running through your mind. Seeing the end result so clearly: you lying on the floor with your wrists cut wide open and the stain of blood lasting as long as the pain everyone has caused you.

And having your mom come in from a date with a man who you heard was married, a man she always claimed was a friend. And you ask her, "Are you sleeping with him?" Then having your mom answer in a matter of fact tone, "Yes, I am."

Then running into the other room to get your suitcase so you can return to your husband, a husband who may also be sleeping with someone else. And while you're taking that twenty-minute drive you feel like you're going crazy, screaming at the top of your lungs because you don't know what else to do, you can't get all that hurt out of you. So you scream and keep screaming until you're back at your apartment parking lot.

Or you're working at a job with a woman named Pam who's having an affair with a married man. His wife is pregnant with their second child, and Pam claims she's saving the marriage because she remembers when she was pregnant she didn't want to have sex, so she was just stepping in and helping out. And all you can think about is what about just not having sex while his wife is pregnant? And what about the marriage vows? Why doesn't that guarantee faithfulness?

And remembering because Pam was so willing to help out, one day he decided his brother needed help too. So they both went over to her house and had sex with her together. Both men were married. You have to hear this at work, then go home to your abusive husband, who also has brothers. Then you have to question your own marriage vows. So one day you realize you've grown strong and you leave. You leave your husband, your mom, and you leave the Pams of your life behind you. And when you choose to start over with your new life, you realize your strength is actually calluses and purple scars that will always be there.

I came out of those thoughts and memories wishing things had been different for me, wishing things would be different for women. Wishing my scars and calluses were really the strength I had originally thought they were.

I sat up and wiped my eyes. I could hear laughter in the other room and decided that's probably what I needed. I stood, stretched, and quickly folded the blanket I had used.

I opened the door and the light coming from the kitchen made me squint. I entered the bathroom and turned on the light. I sat to use the toilet, while my eyes adjusted.

I looked into the mirror to check my hair and face so it wouldn't look so obvious that I had just awakened. Looking at myself in the mirror, I noticed little wrinkles by my eyes and how my skin didn't look tight anymore. For the first time, I saw an anger and hurt on my face that was my natural relaxed expression. Smiling didn't even remove it completely.

I carry my past around with me, all my hurts and anger. When I was young, I was a victim. But now, I'm twenty-seven, old enough and strong enough to look at my life and make changes. I don't want to feel like a victim anymore. I want to fight back.

Chapter 54

I WAS SHOCKED when I joined the crowd. Almost all the girls from the club were there in the kitchen. They had gotten every chair from the house into the one room. I couldn't believe it, and I was upset I was missing it. I looked at the clock hanging above the refrigerator; it was three-thirty in the morning. I sneaked in and sat on the only stool left; it was holding an ashtray. I moved it and suddenly realized they were planning to take over the strip club.

I was nervous with anticipation, but I couldn't understand how this could be happening. I knew Julie was a big part behind the whole thing, ever since that night at the club when I mentioned it. The women were willing to lose their jobs and maybe go to jail. I could not decide how I felt about it. It would be great to show men what they do to us, but at the same time I didn't want to see these women get hurt, although they were already hurt by what they were doing. Maybe losing their jobs would be the best thing for them. It might push them to go for the flower shop.

It seemed I came in at the end of it. Too tired to say anything, I just listened. They were talking about how they could get guns and some of the women were discussing other friends of theirs who would be interested in being a part of it. More or less the conversation was about how they could pull it off, who would do what, and what the outcome would be. Mainly they were laughing about the result.

How they would be in control of the men, how they would be making fun of them, and putting them down. How great it would feel to have that kind of power. How they would like to humiliate them and take away part of their spirit just like they had been doing to us for so many years. A rough game plan was established, but I thought at the time that it was just fantasy talk. Knowing Julie, I should have known better.

Chapter 55

JULIE AND I were cleaning up, both a little crabby and overtired.

"Boy, we were all a bunch of men bashers weren't we?" I asked.

"Men deserve to be bashed!" Julie said.

"I hate the thought of men sitting around talking about women in a derogatory way, but yet here we were, all talking about them."

"I know, Angie, what you mean, but this stuff is all true. Men, not women, abused these women. We are treated like inferiors compared to men. You know it as well as I do," she said.

"I know you're right," I said.

"So. Are you coming over tomorrow night?" she asked.

"You guys aren't really going through with this are you? They really want to do this?" I asked.

"I don't know if we'll pull it off, but we're going to try. And don't sound so surprised. It was your idea. Anyway, we're meeting here tomorrow night. It's the slowest night at the club, and most of the girls have the night off. You're coming, right?"

I hesitated "I don't know… Yeah, I'll be here."

"We're going to tape record the meeting for the girls who can't make it."

"Kay is the only one who won't have anything to do with it, but she said she won't tell either. She has Thursdays off so that's the night we have planned. Either this Thursday or next," she said.

"We're still going to the 'Take Back The Night' march tonight, right?" I asked.

"Yeah."

"Do you mind if I invite a friend to come with us? I want you to meet him."

"Yeah, that'd be great!" She said. "Who is he?"

"That artist, Trayn, I met at the coffee shop with Veronica."

"Oh, that's right, thu Vommmpire," she said, trying to be scary.

I laughed. "That's the one. He asked me to go with him before I even told him I was going. I figured if he's going and we're going, we may as well go together."

"Should we all meet someplace or…"

"Would it be OK if we all meet at my office?"

"You're going in today?" she asked.

"Yes. I have to get started on some new ideas."

"That'll work. The march starts about a block away from there anyway."

"Yes. How about five forty-five? I think it starts at six." I said. "I'm going to tell Trayn five-thirty. I think he likes to be late."

"I'll come at five-thirty too. Maybe we can talk about some of those ideas."

"Thanks, I could use the help. Here's three I have. One is a follow up to my last but interviewing the men."

"Buzzzz!" Julie buzzed the wrong answer.

"My second idea is something to do with Trayn." I waited for a 'buzz' but she didn't say anything. "My third is to somehow get into the women's prison system, maybe as a prisoner myself and get some of the women's stories. I'm interested in knowing how they ended up there."

"Ding! Ding! Ding! That's the winner!"

I smiled. "You think so?"

"Definitely!"

"Oh, it's going to be hard work."

"Anything worth having is," she said.

"I'll see you at five-thirty."

"See ya!"

Chapter 56

BEFORE THE MARCH, we had several speakers. To my surprise, Trayn was one of them.

He walked up to the mike. "Hi, my name is Trayn. I'm very happy to see all of the men who came out here tonight to support this event. We need to help each other!"

Everyone started clapping.

"I'm here tonight because I have a story to tell. When I was thirteen I lost both my parents to domestic abuse. See, my mother shot and killed my father. I blamed my mother. I hated her. I lost my mother because I left that day and never spoke to her again until twelve years later when she was dying of cancer. She died just after I found out the truth about my parents. My father would have killed my mother, but she had enough strength to save herself. She killed him before he could kill her. She had taken abuse for years, and the only reason she felt she deserved to live was because of the strong and wonderful women at the shelters."

Everybody cheered, clapped and whistled.

"That's not where my story ends," he said quieting the audience. "I'm my parents' product." Trayn started crying. "I put my last girlfriend in the hospital for three months."

Julie and I shared a look of concern.

"That was four years ago. I want to tell you about her... She was beautiful. She was about this tall." He held his hand to himself showing she came just to his chest. "She came to my heart," he said. "She was so delicate… I remember her beautiful hands. Her hands and her heart were so full of passion. She was a pianist, on her way to fame. One night she came home from a concert she had given. She was late. Therefore, I had plenty of time to imagine she was with another man. When she came home I broke every one of her fingers." Trayn closed his eyes and put his head down.

He looked back up and his tears started coming again. "Today her hands are so crippled she can't play anymore. She says she still has a rewarding life. She teaches music, and she is raising our four-year-old boy. She gave birth to him when she was in the hospital during that three months she was recovering from the abuse I had given her. Our baby was born with ten fingers and ten toes, to my surprise. In other words, healthy. It's weird, she didn't fight much for herself, but boy did she fight for that baby… I wasn't ready to be a father, so when I found out she was pregnant… I tried to give her an abortion with a coat hanger. That time she saved the baby by knocking me out with a clock radio."

There were a couple of claps from the audience.

"Yes," Trayn said agreeing and continued. "When she was a little further along, I remember she was just getting out of the shower. I walked into the bathroom and stood there with my hands behind my back. I watched her dry off. She was so pretty, her belly was getting big. She looked like an angel, and I hated her for it. She kept smiling at me like she thought I had a surprise for her. I did… I had a can of very flammable bug spray in my hand and when she was dry, I soaked her with it. The fumes alone made her vomit, and I started her on fire. I remember her on fire, holding her stomach as she turned on the shower water and crawled in. She was burned on the right side of her back and shoulder."

Everyone listened in silence, most of us were crying.

"The list goes on and on. Until she left me. That's when it stopped. That is when it stops. That's all you can do is get out. It is the only way to stop it. I made all the promises, telling her I'd never do it again, begging her to give me another chance. Even if I didn't hit her for awhile, the abuse was always there in some form." Trayn looked down again.

"I've gotten a lot of help, but to this day I don't trust myself to have a relationship with someone. I never want to do the things I've done to her to another. Now I just try to live day by day in hopes that one-day I can make it up to my son and to his mother, but I know I never can. And I pray my son learns from his mother and me to respect people, to respect women, but mostly to respect himself so he can respect others. He's a good boy." Trayn started crying again. "His mother is doing a great job raising him and showing him that she, as a woman, as a human being, deserves respect. I know that if she had stayed with me she never could have done that. She is strong. She gave us all a gift when she left me and pressed charges and put me in jail. But most importantly… " He paused and looked around to all of us. "She broke the cycle."

Everyone clapped and wiped their eyes.

"Maybe a story about him isn't such a bad idea," Julie yelled over the applause.

"I don't think so," I answered.

Trayn walked back over to us. "I'm sorry to spring it all on you like this."

I didn't want to be judgmental, but I didn't see Trayn the same way. It was hard for me to see him as a kind man after hearing about how he used to be a monster. A part of me hated him.

Chapter 57

AFTER THE MARCH, Julie had to check on getting guns for the club takeover. I went along and waited in the car. The alley was dark and dirty. There was one light at the top of a crooked wooded stairway. It seemed there were apartments upstairs. There was a parking area with spray-painted numbers on the brick wall in front of each space. Graffiti covered the green garbage dumpsters. How ironic I thought: we just marched for nonviolence, and now I'm getting guns with Julie.

She came back to the car with a heavy cardboard box. She struggled to get it in the back seat. She got in and started the car.

"What's that?" I asked.

"The guns."

"You're kidding. Don't you think you should put them in the trunk? Are they legal?" I asked frantically.

She turned around and opened the box.

I turned around and looked in. There were about twenty handguns. "Oh, my God!" I turned back around to the front window. "I'm out of this!"

"Angie, look," she said grabbing, one of the guns.

"Yes. I know what a gun looks like." I didn't look. I could see she was pointing the gun to the windshield.

She pulled the trigger. "BANG!" The gun went off.

I turned toward her. "What the fuck do you think you're doing!" I demanded.

She pointed to the window, which didn't have a bullet hole in it. "Angie, they're blanks!"

"I don't care!" I screamed over the buzzing in my ears.

She turned the car off. "Angie, you know me better than that," she said gently. "What's going on with you?"

"You scared me," I said. I could smell the gun fire.

"I'm sorry. I didn't mean to. Do you want to talk about it?"

I exhaled and unloaded. "I'm upset about the things Trayn did. I'm upset about the women there tonight who have been abused. I'm upset I've been abused. I'm upset because of how women are treated. But mostly I'm upset because women keep letting it happen for whatever fuckin' reason."

"Angie, what Trayn did is in the past. Besides, things are getting better."

I started crying. "No, they're not! Things are not getting better! And I don't know how to make things better," I said.

"You're doing your part, Ang."

"It's not enough."

"That's why we're doing this," she said holding the gun up. "We're going to make a huge statement with this. It'll be on the news all across the states. I don't care if I go to jail. If this gets the ball rolling, women will follow our lead and start fighting back, demanding respect."

"People get respect when they deserve it, not demand it," I said.

"Yes, but men don't give us the chance to deserve it; they don't believe we deserve it, and they won't until we demand it. Once we get it, then we can show them we deserved it all along," Julie said. "Besides in this man's world, the men get the respect by being toughest in sports, business and whatever else. So now we're going to play by their rules, not by going along and giving them what they want from women, but fighting fire with their fire."

I agreed with most of what she was saying and decided to fight along with her. I knew Julie would never be a part of hurting anyone. "I can't believe you got all these guns," I said reaching to look in the box.

"I know. The guy needed some heavy convincing. He's in the gun business and his pawn shop is right next to it." She looked in the box with me. "We have Berretta, Taurus, Bersa, all 22s."

"So what, we're all going to have blanks in our guns?" I asked.

"Yes, all except me. I'm going to have my gun in case we have problems. But I don't want any of the others to know, for their protection. If the police show up, I want them to be innocent. I'll be the only one who could get in trouble that is more serious. There's going to be a lot of emotions, adrenaline flowing that night. I don't want anyone to be tempted to make a mistake.

"That's a good idea," I said. "I can't believe this!"

"Yeah, I know. A couple of things we need to remember. These guns are still very dangerous. The gunpowder at close range could still penetrate... kill. And I got some Chloroform to knock the guys out. It takes about five to ten seconds, and I know they will fight. We have to have at least three girls on these guys to take em' down. I know Veronica is strong, and Jody, but we need others who are willing to fight a man and win."

It was getting serious. Something inside me was stirring with excitement, but I was also scared.

"Remind me of this stuff at our next get together. We'll make the final arrangements for the takeover." She started the car to take me home. "You'll be there, right?"

"Yeah, I'll be there."

Chapter 58

WELL, THIS WAS it. Julie and her group were around back and another group was in the front. In about ten minutes, this whole thing was going down. I was sitting at a table alone. My bag was on my lap with my gun inside.

I could see the nervous anticipation in the dancers and servers. For about the last half-hour, random dancers had asked for help from the male workers and bouncers. They would take them in back; Julie and a couple girls knocked them out with chloroform, tied them up, taped their mouths, and locked them in different rooms. There were only a few male workers left on the floor; the DJ, who we needed to play the music, two bouncers, and one of the owners behind the counter where you first walk in. Sara was doing a great job keeping him occupied. I could not believe how well this was going, probably better than planned.

The last two bouncers were off the floor, and it was time. Rebecca was the first one I saw coming through the front doors with the group of girls following her. I stood and noticed Julie's group coming in from the rear. All I could do was stand and smile, practically laughing. The men looked around as if this were some kind of special attraction, not realizing *they* were soon to be the attraction.

Julie was at the microphone. She popped off a couple shots into the air and asked for everyone's attention. "How ya'll doing tonight?" she hollered into the mike as if she was DJing for an exciting event. "I hope you're having a great night because we have a special treat for you! OK now gentlemen, or should I say pigs, I want you to take me serious because I do have a gun and so does every woman in the place."

The women pulled out their guns and held them high.

"We have both the front and rear doors blocked. So just sit back, enjoy the ride, and nobody will be hurt. Any questions? OK, now I'd like you all to take out your wallets and place them on the table in front of you. The women will be around to pick them up. Don't worry you'll get them back. We're not here to cause problems. We just want to have a little fun, that's all. So if you cooperate, you'll leave here with everything you came in with, plus maybe a different outlook on this whole environment that you've allowed yourself to enter. If you don't, let's just say you may run into trouble, and it doesn't end with us telling your wives everything we know about you. Take your wallets out NOW!"

I noticed someone walking up onto the stage. It was Trayn. He looked different, not so vampirish. He was attractive. I, along with everyone, watched him step next to Julie. I felt anger that Trayn would hang out at a place like this. But it soon turned to pure entertainment when he grabbed for the mike and Julie wouldn't let him have it. I realized it was an act they planned. They both had a hold of the mike. I heard Julie yell, "Let go, you cock sucker!"

"No! You girls can't do this!" he hollered back still struggling for the mike.

Suddenly, Veronica hopped onto the stage. Standing next to Trayn, she pointed her gun toward his chest and pulled the trigger. Fake blood splattered across his body and onto Julie as Trayn fell to the ground. Julie and Veronica both looked down at him then to each other and did a quick hand-slap like a high five. I heard Julie say, "Thanks" from the mike. Veronica grabbed a hold of Trayn's legs and pulled him off to the side behind Julie and the DJ. Julie stood wiping the blood from her face and she yelled with anger, "Where are the fuckin' wallets?"

The men looked around to see if the other men were doing as they were instructed, and they all started reaching for their wallets. There was a girl in every area to make sure they did so. I started collecting them on my way to the stage. I approached two men, the rudest in the crowd that night and many other nights I was there. With my gun in hand I said to the dark-haired husky guy, "Take your clothes off!" I turned to the shorter blonde and said, "You take your clothes off, too."

They both refused, and I heard Julie say, "Are you having problems with those two, Ang? Are you going to make another example of them?"

"I guess so," I hollered back. I cocked and pointed my gun at them.

Their clothes came off quickly, all except their underwear. I told them that was OK to start with, and I escorted them to the stage. Julie was getting the DJ to spin the music without any trouble; he seemed impressed with this whole thing, because I caught him chuckling a few times. The guys were standing there looking embarrassed and ashamed. The music was playing, and I told them to dance and remove their underwear in a sexy manner. Two more guys were walking up onto the stage. They were completely naked, and I looked out to the rest of the club and most of the men were naked and waiting their turns to dance, not because they wanted to, but because we were making them. I walked to the opposite side of the dance floor from Julie and the DJ to stand back and watch. By this time, the girls were really getting into it. They were waving the money they took from their wallets, laughing, and putting the men down.

There were skinny men, fat men, old men, young men, pale and dark men, all naked for us to watch and say whatever we pleased. Surprisingly enough, most of them had very small penises.

"If you want the money you came in with, you gotta work for it. Come on guys you can dance better than that, let's see those asses," Julie said from the mike. "You've been here enough, you know how it's done! Who wants a lap dance?"

All the girls yelled, "I do!" and raised their hands.

Julie laughed into the mike.

The guys really weren't dancing much, just standing there. A few were, though, only because the gun was a little closer. All the men were helpless; we took all their clothes, all their money, and identification, plus we held guns, laughing at them.

"And we're not a bunch of women suffering from PMS," Julie said. "We just want you to know how it feels. How does it feel, guys? Do you like it?"

Rebecca got up on stage and took the mike from Julie. Julie stepped back anxious to hear what she had to say. "You! Come over here! Let me see your cock. Oh, that's a nice cock. Can you get it hard for me? Ooh, you got me so horny! And you," she pointed to an older, out of shape man, "Come here! Bend over and grab your ankles, I wanna see that saggy elephant ass. Do it now!" He did. So she continued, "Oh, look at that ass."

I couldn't believe she was talking like that, but it was the same way, these same men had talked to them. One man was standing at the back of the stage not dancing. He kept edging his way toward Trayn. I was concerned he might be a doctor and find out that Trayn wasn't really shot. Veronica must have felt the same way. She ran up to him and put the gun to his head. He fell to his knees and started crying. "Why aren't you dancing?" Veronica demanded.

"I... I... " He lowered his head and kept crying.

"You what!"

"I'm... sorry. I'm sorry..." His face was bright red and his bald head was glistening from sweat.

"Yeah? What are you sorry for?"

He just kept crying.

"You're a fuckin' coward, you know that?" She slapped him on the back of the head and left him there, on his knees crying.

As I watched, I became overwhelmed with anger. I lowered my gun and stood there, saddened by all that was taking place. I glanced through the crowd, amazed at how cooperative the men were without their clothes. I was failing to find the differences between men and women.

I saw a man approaching the stage. I thought he had taken one of the women's guns and was going to try to be a hero. He moved to the stage, toward Julie and Rebecca. I knew they would take care of it. I wanted to laugh at his cockiness until he flashed them his badge. Then I recognized him. It was the cop, who had raped Rebecca. I knew our fun was over. I heard Julie say, "Shit!" into the mike as she lowered it.

He was trying to escort Rebecca off the stage, but Julie wouldn't let him take her. They weren't moving. Everyone was standing there watching the three argue but not being able to hear what they were saying, the music was too loud. Suddenly Rebecca was hit hard across the face by the back of his hand, causing her to fall off the stage and into several naked men standing there.

I could see Julie's anger matched my own. I quickly walked toward them ditching men on the way. I kept my eyes on Julie and her gun. I was scared of what she might be tempted to do, especially if she knew this cop had raped Rebecca. When I reached them they were still arguing, Julie still had her gun on him and his gun was on her. The DJ was trying to help. "Come on man, put your gun down. They're not hurting anybody. Just let them finish."

"No, stay the fuck out of this!" the cop yelled, flushed, panicky.

The DJ stopped the music and continued. "These guys deserve this. Come on man; put your gun down. Just walk out of here. Nobody will ever know you were here." He turned to Julie; "Julie let him walk out of here."

The cop was looking toward Julie for her answer.

Julie answered, "Hell, no! He's staying!" She pointed to his hand. "He only wants to go to protect himself. So his wife doesn't find out where he spends his time." I noticed Julie and DJ looking down at his wedding band. Rebecca was right; he was married.

Julie looked at me, then with disgust at him, and said, "To protect and serve. Oh, wait! But it's different now isn't it?" she said to the cop. "Help us help you, right?"

Rebecca was back up on the stage holding her face. "I guess you should have hit me a little harder, you didn't knock me out. And you're not going to shut me up this time," she said. She turned to Julie and cried out, "He raped me."

Julie flared with anger. "What!"

Rebecca turned back to the cop and pointed to her face. "This is nothing compared to last time you put your hands on me."

"What are you talking about? I would never touch you. You're a slut!"

She ignored him and continued. "It was about a month ago. Some of us hung around after we closed. There'd been a drunk here and a few cops were hanging around."

DJ interrupted, "I remember that night. I was going to give you a ride home; your car was in the shop."

"That's right, you were here. Anyway I wanted to go home, and you weren't ready to go. So he," pointing to the cop, "was about to get off duty and head back to the station. He offered me a ride. I accepted. He raped me in his squad car."

"You're crazy. You only wish I'd touch you."

Ignoring him again, she went on, "After it happened he threatened to throw me in jail if I told anyone. For what, I don't know, but it scared me enough to keep my mouth shut. He told me he could set me up in an hour, and I'd be in jail."

Julie turned her gun to his groin.

"Julie don't!" I yelled.

The cop lowered his gun and used it to cover himself.

"I am so sick of above-the-law cops. You think your badge gives you access to everything. I got news for you. It doesn't!" She was enraged. "You're going to jail." She cocked her gun, still pointed at his groin. "Confess!"

He was scared and sweat was pouring off him. "OK, I did it, but it won't stick," he said. "My wife was out of town, so I figured I'd have some fun with her." He pointed to Rebecca. "The bitch didn't want to, so I took it. Big fuckin' deal!"

Rebecca, who was standing right in front of me, pointed her gun at him and shot several times. Yelling, "You Fucker!"

He shot back.

***

I attempted to raise my hand to feel my head, but I started to fall in what seemed like slow motion. I could feel every joint give on my way down. There was nothing in my way to fall against: not a chair, table, or person around to catch me. My body hit the floor. It didn't hurt until my head hit. Blood seemed to squirt from the front of my face. I lay still, my tears mixing with my blood seemed natural to me, comforted me.

Everything turned black and fuzzy. A comfortable pinching released my entire body. I went back in time.

I was on my hands and knees crawling, trying to get away from my mad husband. He was behind me grabbing at me, trying to keep me. I was groaning and crying in panic, moving away from him as quickly as I could. I felt his fist strike the back of my head so hard my face hit the floor in front of me. I lay on my living room floor where he left me, crying. The pain in the front of my head now matched that of the back. My tears wouldn't stop. I knew how it worked. He hit me either on my head so my hair would cover the bruises or on my body in places where my clothes would hide the pain I endured. I couldn't understand why this was happening, why it was so easy for him to do this to me. I couldn't move. I couldn't get up from this low place I had fallen to. I lay there wishing I were dead; wishing he had hit me a little harder, hard enough to kill me. He didn't; he hit me just hard enough to hurt me, to let me know he was in control. Two hours earlier he had told me he loved me.

I regained consciousness for a moment. I wasn't on the floor in my living room and the burning in my head was not from my husband's fist. I tried to sit up. Oh, my God! Oh, my God… what happened? Oh, my God, what happened to me? My head! My head! I opened my burning eyes to bright lights flashing. As if I was under water, I heard commotion in the room. I wasn't sure where I was.

Suddenly Julie was next to me. She was holding my hand, trying to wipe the blood from my face. She was crying and telling me everything was going to be all right. I could tell it was bad. She was so strong, and I'd never seen her like this. She turned her head and screamed, "Get a fuckin' ambulance… NOW!"

"Jul, what did I do… what happened?" I whispered.

"Angie. Angie you've been shot."

After a long silence, I stammered, "By a… by a man?" I gave her a grim smile and I felt my body go cold. I started convulsing and everything went dark and silent.

Chapter 59

IN THE HOSPITAL, it was quiet and still. I no longer heard the commotion. I tried to open my eyes feeling confident the whole thing had been a dream.

My life played out before me more like a sad movie than the life I had hoped for. My memories came to me the same way I'd ramble them off to the many counselors I'd gone to, always trying to keep them in chronological order. This time they mixed with pain and forgotten details.

Julie's voice pulled me out of my memories. I could see her talking to my body. My best friend was sitting next to me on my bed, but it wasn't really me anymore. She was not crying. She was just sitting there, staring at me.

"I don't know what's going to happen to you, my friend, but I can't help wishing it were me lying in that bed," she said. "I know I'm the one who kinda pushed you into this whole thing, and you're the one who got shot. You're the one lying there. It never shoulda happened. I never thought something like this would happen. Angie, we've always been straight with each other, so I have to tell you something… It's bad, really bad. I can't forget you lying there. Angie, that cop shot you in the head. After I heard the shot I looked over at you and saw you go down. I had no idea it was so bad until I got to you."

"During the investigation he said it was an accident. Me and Rebecca are going to see to it he not only loses his badge but he goes to prison for a long time. I can't believe that guy was a cop." She exhaled deeply and continued. "I don't even know exactly what happened. I know we never meant to hurt anybody, it just got out of hand. You're the only one who got shot. After he shot you he turned his gun on Rebecca, and that's when I ran to be next to you." She started crying, "Ang, you've got to come out of this. You wouldn't believe Rebecca. She stood there. She saw you go down. She was screaming. His gun was pointed right at her. So she couldn't go to you. She begged him to shoot her, too. And Trayn, he's having a really hard time. He's coming to see you today." She sniffed, "Oh, Angie, I don't know what I'd do without you... go ahead, rest up, take your time, but please come back to us. We have to finish what we started!"

I lay there, wishing I had more time with her as the realization of my condition was sinking in. She was a strong woman, and I was proud to be her friend.

Chapter 60

MY LIFE CARRIED a feeling of love, almost rapture, through me, made me warm, made me light. Feeling nothing, was I loved? Then feeling love again for the people who loved me.

I knew time was close. I could feel it. I didn't want to go yet. The weight of time held me down.

I wanted to… I want to love; I want to be loved. I want to see my mom again. I want to see my family and my sisters. I want to talk to Julie and all my new friends. Please. Not yet. Please. I never found the one to love, the one who would love me! Come on, give me another chance. Please. Give me another chance.

I was lying there. Close to death. Begging and crying for more time. And time was lying on me, flowing over me, running off me.

I won't be afraid anymore, I promise, please, just give me the chance! I want to be loved; I want to be loved please. PLEASE! I want to be loved! I didn't give anyone that chance to love me, please.

I had been killed by a man. Another man killed me, my spirit. My spirit killed over and over again by men my whole life, and a man had finally taken the last of it out of me. Why?

I'm going… Oh God, I don't want to go… Julie… Mom!

A comforting numb came over me and everything started to slow. My memories. My tears. My heartbeat. I was light, if I moved I'd float. I wanted to float. I was not afraid. I moved my arms slightly and began to rise to brightness, as if stepping out into the daylight from a dark room, a room I'd been in my whole life. When I opened my eyes it was like opening them for the first time, like being born with an understanding, a clarity about my life I had never seen before. Pain disappeared. My tears dried, and I was taken over by a feeling of love I'd never known but had always wanted.

I was lifted and cradled in what seemed to be arms, strong arms, wrapped around me holding me, not masculine or feminine, not male or female, just a powerful presence of love embracing me. I could see nothing but felt everything. I cried hard. I had been searching my whole life for this, and it wasn't anything outside of me. It was something inside I had stuffed away for protection. Now protection was no longer needed. I was in a safe place.

Chapter 61

A WARM, TINGLING light sensation filled me. I was no longer my body. It was a completely different container with no walls, no constrictions. Shapes began to come my way. I couldn't make them out. I closed my eyes, hoping for better focus. It worked. When I opened them, my grandma was floating over me.

She sat down next to me and held my hand. I could feel her warmth. She didn't say a word. I knew this woman sitting beside me was the strength behind my family.

"Oh, Grandma." I started to cry. "I'm so sorry. I was afraid of you. I was afraid of what you knew about me. I was such a coward, the way I treated you in the hospital when you had your first stroke. Your strength overwhelms me, and now as I lie here and the tables are turned, I'm already afraid of what you're going to say to me. Probably, 'I love you.' The same, 'I love you' I should have said to you. But I didn't. I just cried about how bad *my* life was, how bad *I* had it. I had to unload all my garbage on you. You, Grandma, you just had a stroke. I can't believe how selfish I was.

"Then when you recovered I couldn't talk to you. I felt such guilt. I was embarrassed. God, Grandma why'd I do that to you?"

"Angie, don't cry." My grandma whispered as she wiped my tears. "I know you think you made a mistake when you cried to me, but it was a gift. You did me a favor. I didn't think it was important if I lived or died, until you came into my room to say goodbye. You were crying as you brushed my hair and at that moment I knew I was needed, I wanted to stay alive for you. I knew you were in for some hard times. I also knew I was the only one who knew about it. Angie, you needed me, and I'm so thankful for that. I lived to see my great grandchildren, I helped my husband through his open-heart surgery, and I watched you become such a strong woman. You left your abusive husband, and I like to think I helped you when you needed it most.

"Now it's your turn to do something for me. I need you to go back. You are too young. You have too much to live for. Angie, don't be so afraid to let a man love you. A good man wants to love you."

With one hand on my arm and the other rubbing my forehead, she watched me reconnect with my body. "OK, I'll go back, Grandma. I'll go back."

About the Author

Becky Due is the new voice of women's fiction. She has the courage, honesty and writing style for today's busy women, and she does not cringe away from hard issues. She will leave you feeling strong, self-confident, independent, and in control of your life.

Her books have won and been finalists in several independent competitions including the 2010 and 2011 National Indie Excellence Awards, USA Book News and the 2009 IPPY Awards.

Other Great Titles by Becky Due

The Gentlemen's Club: A Story for All Women (Novel)

Touchable Love: An Untraditional Love Story (Novel)

Returning Injury: A Suspense Celebrating Women's Strength (Novel)

The Dumpster: One Woman's Search for Love (Novel)

Traveling for Love: Searching for Self, Hoping for Love (Novel)

Blue the Bird: On Flying (Children's)

**The Woman's Handbook: Everything You Want To Say To Your
Daughter, Sister, Niece, Friend In One Simple Book
(Gift Book/Self-Help)**

2 Days to Healthy Self-Esteem (Self-Help)

I'm Upset! App for Women (App)

Visit Becky Due at

www.BeckyDue.com
http://www.facebook.com/BeckyDue.Author
www.twitter.com/BeckyDue

www.ingramcontent.com/pod-product-compliance
Lightning Source LLC
Chambersburg PA
CBHW020944180626
46814CB00003B/922